HERE TODAY, GONE TOMORROW 2

Lock Down Publications and Ca$h
Presents

Here Today Gone Tomorrow 2

A Novel by *Fly Rock*

Lock Down Publications
Po Box 944
Stockbridge, Ga 30281

Visit our website @
www.lockdownpublications.com

Here Today Gone Tomorrow 2

First Edition July 2023
Printed in the United States of America

Lock Down Publications
Like our page on Facebook: Lock Down Publications @
www.facebook.com/lockdownpublications.ldp
Book interior design by: **Shawn Walker**
Edited by: **Kiera Northington**

Stay Connected with Us!

Text **LOCKDOWN** to 22828 to stay up-to-date with new releases, sneak peaks, contests and more…
Thank you.

Submission Guideline.

Submit the first three chapters of your completed manuscript to ldpsubmissions@gmail.com, subject line: Your book's title. The manuscript must be in a .doc file and sent as an attachment. Document should be in Times New Roman, double spaced and in size 12 font. Also, provide your synopsis and full contact information. If sending multiple submissions, they must each be in a separate email.

Have a story but no way to send it electronically? You can still submit to LDP/Ca$h Presents. Send in the first three chapters, written or typed, of your completed manuscript to:

LDP: Submissions Dept
Po Box 944
Stockbridge, Ga 30281

DO NOT send original manuscript. Must be a duplicate.

Provide your synopsis and a cover letter containing your full contact information.

Thanks for considering LDP and Ca$h Presents.

Special Thanks / Acknowledgements

Back at it again! I got to give a special thanks and shout-out to the CEO. This opportunity is a privilege and a blessing…

Shout out to my baby, Ashley, for assisting me with my decision making. You green as fuck, but I love you though! Lol…

Super shout-out to Wizz and Bo-T! Without the brotherly bond them niggas realistically created this book wouldn't be possible…

Shout-out to the rest of my friends and family, and of course, shout-out to the Armor truck! This is Rock Star talent!

Chapter 1

Everything was black but I could feel my heart beating.

Am I dead? Before I could answer my thoughts, I heard a female's voice talking over me.

"Why do you want me to keep babysitting this grown ass man? You act like I ain't got shit to do!" the female spoke.

"Dora, please..." another woman whined. "I need to go to work. He probably won't even wake up tonight. So far, he's only opened his eyes twice since he's been here, and both times he was too drugged up to speak. Please just stay in the house until I get back."

"I don't even understand why you keep this man here anyway. Take his ass to the damn hospital with you."

"I can't, Dora, I told you that."

"Yeah, you keep saying you can't, but why the hell not? You ain't told me shit I wanna know yet! Like, who the fuck is this man? Where the hell did he come from and why the hell is he here?"

"Dora, I told you...it's complicated and I don't know how to explain it all—"

"How about the fucking truth, Tori! Tell me the truth or I I'm leaving! This is the second time you have asked me to do this shit, and you have yet to ease my mind about it!"

The two women went silent for a moment and eventually the voice that belonged to Tori said, "Okay, okay...Look, just sit tight this one more time and when I come back, I promise to tell you everything."

"But you don't even have to work tonight," Dora complained.

"I know, but his IV bag is getting low, and I need to get him some more morphine."

"Sounds like all the more reason to take his ass with you!"

"Dora! Are you going to stay or not?" Tori questioned.

Dora sighed and said, "Alright, I'll watch him, damn! You could've picked a better night to bore me to death though. He at least could've been up. Then he might've been able to make his fine ass useful."

"Yeah, well, tough luck…Thank you though…I'll be back sometime tomorrow morning" Tori spoke. She then quickly stepped out of the room before her only friend and had time to rethink her decision.

I continued to stay there in the darkness while thinking about the conversation I just heard.

Who are these people?

Where the fuck am I even at?

It then occurred to me the reason behind the darkness was because my eyes were still closed. I kept them closed for about another ten minutes while silently listening to my surroundings.

Silence.

When I finally opened my eyes, the sudden brightness caused me to immediately shut them.

Damn!

I slowly opened them again and allowed my vision to adjust to the light. I took in my surroundings and was completely dumbfounded.

Where the fuck am I at?

I was lying in a twin sized bed I'm sure I've never been in, inside of a bedroom I'm sure I've never seen. I had an IV needle stuck in my arm and the tube was attached to a pole pumping a clear fluid into my veins. My shoulder was patched up with a white pad and tape and my left leg was wrapped up in a band and covered with a splint. I was wearing a hospital gown, but I was clearly not in a hospital.

Where the fuck am I at?

I stared at the roof and tried to think and that's when it hit me! So many memories flooded me at one time, it was nearly impossible to process them all. I took a deep breath and closed my eyes again. I could vividly see myself staring down at the MAC-90 in my lap. When I looked up, we crashed!

Hold on…Where the fuck Bo-T at?

Damn…Just keep thinking…

What happened next?

I remembered crawling out the window of the upside-down Bentley truck and dragging the MAC-90. Behind me, Bo-T was laying in the median of the highway, getting punched by that federal agent who was chasing us. I remember using all of my might to lift the MAC-90 and when I pulled the trigger, I ripped the agent in half.

Me and Bo-T stole his Jaguar and then fled the scene,

Then what happened?

I can't remember…

Think, Wize, think…

Okay, somehow, I ended up at a hospital. I was standing by myself in front of a hospital with two duffles hanging around my neck.

Hold up…My money!

Where the fuck my bags at?

I quickly re-opened my eyes and frantically looked around the room.

Nothing!

My bags were nowhere to be seen.

Fuck!

Did I get robbed?

Naw.

A woman came out of the hospital, and I forced her to take me somewhere. She said she was a doctor.

Is that where I'm at?

One of the two chicks sounded like she may have been a doctor, the one that had to go to work. Last thing I remember is getting in the car with the lady. Nothing else…

Fuck all that…where the fuck my money at? I need to get the fuck up out of here. I gotta find Bo-T.

I ended my thoughts and sat up in bed, and immediately felt a jolt of pain rush through my shoulder. I fought the urge to scream and slowly eased my legs down. They felt numb and like a dead weight. When my feet made contact with the soft carpet, I took another look around the room, but this time I made a more detailed inspection.

There was a bag of cotton balls and other wound care supplies on a dresser directly to my left, so I decided to make use of them. I've had more than enough doctor visits in my life to know how to handle minor things.

I ripped off a piece of tape and stuck it to the back side of my hand. I then took a cotton ball and held it over my arm where the IV punctured me. I pulled the tape off that held the IV in place and slowly slid the needle from my arm. I let the needle and tubing drop to the floor, and then covered the small red dot that appeared on my arm with the cotton ball. I used the tape on the back of my hand to hold the cotton ball and then I started out my sore arms. Another jolt of pain ripped through my shoulder, but it wasn't that bad.

I looked down at my legs and my whole left thigh was wrapped up, but the splint was around my knee, and it caused my leg to keep uncomfortably straight.

Why the fuck was my knee in a splint if I got shot in the thigh?

I slowly removed the straps from the splint and let the splint drop to the floor. I bent my leg back and my knee cracked in several places. The crack from my knee felt good but my thigh was on fire. I put my foot back on the floor and took a second to adjust to the pain.

I then looked around again and saw an open door that belonged to a bathroom, and two swing doors I assumed would be a closet. There was a small thirty-six-inch smart TV on another dresser in front of the bed and nothing else that I could see.

I stood to my feet but kept all the pressure on my right leg. I could feel my blood rushing through my aching body, but the pain wasn't as bad as I would have expected.

I could do this.

I went with my first mind and limped over to the closet. I took a deep breath and opened the doors.

Bingo!

Two very familiar big black duffle bags.

Always go with your first mind.

I dragged both bags over by the bed and sat back down. I wasn't exactly sure what was in them, amount wise, but I knew what type of content to expect.

I unzipped the first bag and made a quick visual inspection.

Mountains of cocaine.

Field of marijuana.

Bundles of dead presidents.

Beautiful sight!

I unzipped the duffle and unzipped the next one. The second bag was stuffed to the brim with one-hundred-dollar bills. Nothing more, nothing less.

Another beautiful sight!

I re-zipped that bag and sighed deeply.

What a relief…Did the doctor lady even know what I had in my possession? She couldn't have, but then again, she had to.

What type of stranger, under the circumstances of our encounter, wouldn't be curious enough to look inside these bags? Especially if she had to put them in the closet. Did she think it was laundry or something? Of course not.

Shrug.

Oh well, better to just count my blessings. I definitely owe her one. I'll make her a very happy lady.

Hold up…Didn't I have a gun?

"Oh shit! You're up!" a woman screamed from the doorway.

I looked up and was slightly stunned. I didn't expect to see such a beautiful, brown-skinned woman standing in front of me. I tried to finally speak for the first time, but my voice came out cracked and raspy, and I suddenly began to cough uncontrollably.

The brown-skinned woman quickly dashed out of sight without saying a word and left me coughing up my lungs.

What kind of babysitter was this?

I was hunched over, holding my stomach, when she emerged in the room with a bottle of delicious looking water.

"Here, drink this," she quickly spoke and handed me the bottle.

I grabbed the bottle with one hand and kept my other hand clutched against my stomach. I held the bottle towards her, and she quickly removed the cap. I then put the bottle to my lips and took a small sip. That small sip led to one giant chug and in a matter of seconds, I had downed the entire bottle.

Damn!

I took a deep breath and handed the young woman the empty bottle. She accepted the bottle and stared at me with a look of pure curiosity.

I took another deep breath and tried to speak again. The first thing that came out of my mouth was, "Damn!"

She looked at me and didn't respond.

Okay, let me try something that requires a response.

"What's up?"

"Are you okay?" she asked.

"Shit, I guess…I've been worse. Where am I?"

"What do you mean, where are you?"

I looked around the room and answered. "It's a simple question. Where am I? I've never been there before and I'm a little confused."

She tilted her head to the side with a puzzled expression and then for the first time she looked down at my bags.

"Does that belong to you?" she asked me.

"Can we get one question answered before we move onto the next?"

"Okay, I don't know what happened to you, so maybe your injuries fucked your mind up. You're at Tori's house."

"Is that the doctor?"

"Duhhh, don't you know your own doctor?"

"Uh…yeah, right. Alright, now who are you?'

"I'm Tori's friend. She told me to watch you while she went to work."

"What's your name?"

"Does that matter?"

"Of course, it does."

"And why is that?"

"How could I be in the presence of a beautiful woman and not ask her name?"

She turned her head and blushed. When she looked at me again, she said, "My name is Dora. And you are?"

"Wizz."

"Wizz?"

"Yup. So umm, how long have I been here?'

"I don't know. I saw you for the first time a week ago. I had been in the house for like two hours just hanging out and suddenly, I heard someone back here coughing. I looked at Tori like, 'What the fuck is that?' and she rushed back here drank the water and went back to sleep."

"Damn! A week ago? What day is it?"

"February 14th."

"Valentine's Day?'

"Yup."

"What the fuck!" I quickly did the math. "That means I've been here for about three weeks!"

Dora simply looked at me and shrugged.

"So, I take it as my valentine?" I joked.

Dora blushed again and then said, "Where the hell did Tori find you?"

"Long story," I replied.

"I got time."

"I'll let her tell you about it. In the meantime, I really need to get going."

"Going where? How the hell are you gonna leave like that?"

I rose to my feet and said, "Easy. I need to get out of here, and your gonna take me."

She backed up a few steps. "No, the hell I'm not! I was told to watch you, not take you somewhere!"

She put her hands on her soft hips and cocked her head to the side. I couldn't help but smile. I looked down at her bare feet and took notice of her well-manicured toes. I let my eyes come up to her juicy and well-toned brown thighs that poked out slightly at her hips and then curved back in at the waist. Her crop top exposed the flawless brown skin on her belly, and her natural C-cup breasts sat up perfectly, despite the fact that she wasn't wearing a bra. I could see her firm nipples poking through her shirt and when she caught me staring, she covered her round breasts with her hands.

"What the hell are you staring at?" she blurted with a smirk. "For someone who just woke up from a damn near fatal injury, you sure as hell don't seem to have yo mind in the right spot."

I looked at her pouty round lips, her wide and pierced nose, then at her dark brown eyes and smiled. "Quit playing like I ain't hear what you told you homegirl before she left."

She stared into my hazed eyes and looked stunned. "What are you talkin bout?"

"If my memory serves me right, I believe you said something about me making my quote-unquote, 'fine ass' useful," I laughed.

She looked shocked and then smiled. "Whatever, I still ain't taking yo ass nowhere, so you might as well sit yo ass back down and wait on Tori to come back."

I looked down at her five-foot-five body, compared to my five-foot-ten height and then slowly sat back down.

"So, you need some more water?" she asked.

"Yeah, that would be nice. And some Chinese food."

"Chinese food? Where the hell did we get that from?"

"From the Chinese store! Where else do you get Chinese food from? Order it and I'll pay for it."

"You got some money?'

I smiled. "Yup, lots of it."

"Alright, I'ma get you some water and then we'll have some food."

She slowly turned around and exited the room. Her black tights made her booty look like a black bouncy pumpkin and I watched the pumpkin bounce away until it was out of straight.

Once she was gone, I quickly reached in one of my bags and pulled out a handful of hundreds. I tossed the money on the bed and then dragged my two bags back into the closet. Might as well put them back, since it looks like I'm stuck for the moment.

Dora quickly returned with another bottle of water, just as I was sitting back down onto the bed. She handed me the bottle and then noticed the money.

"What the fuck? Where you get all the money from?"

I scooped up the bills and counted out the money I had in my hand, forty-two hundred.

I could see Dora mentally counting the money with me out of the corner of my eye and I could tell she wasn't used to major money.

I counted off a grand and handed it to her. "This chump change, baby. This for you. Payment for your babysitting services. Now can we order that Chinese food? I'm starving."

Chapter 2

When Tori entered her modest, three-bedroom home, it was a little after six in the morning. She wasn't necessarily tired, but she was beyond ready to lay down. The atmosphere in her home was calm as she made her way towards her spacious bedroom.

She tossed her white coat onto her bed and placed her purse on the dresser. She stripped out of her work attire and forced her legs to resist the bed and guide her towards the bathroom. She took a quick shower and then slipped her body into a nightgown.

She went back to her dresser and reached inside her purse, pulled out a bottle of liquid morphine and headed out of the room. She slowly made her way down the hall towards her guest room where she had a complete stranger laid up and began shaking the bottle. She was going to empty the liquid solution into his IV bag in small portions, however often she felt he needed it.

She had been tending to his man for the last three weeks, and she wasn't sure how long this was going to continue. The man wasn't in a coma, he was just extremely out of it. His body had endured a lot of pressure, but he was lucky.

When she got him to her house the night she brought him home, she struggled him out of her car and then dragged his heavy body into her bathroom. He regained consciousness for the moment, so the task was hard but doable. Tori removed the two duffle bags from around his neck and told him to undress himself. She watched him carefully as he wiggled out of his clothes and leaned against her wall.

Tori guided his naked body into her bathtub and turned on some warm water. She used the shower nozzle to spray the caked-up dirt, sweat, and blood away from his body and stared into his eyes. His eyes were beautiful. They were open but distant. He appeared to be staring off into space and she knew his body was on autopilot. He wasn't fully conscious, but he was moving to survive.

Once his body was clean, she realized he had been shot in the shoulder and in the thigh. Lucky for him both bullets had gone in and out. He also had a gash across his forehead and cuts all over his body.

She cleaned each gash and cut, poured alcohol into his open wounds and stitched his shoulder and leg with a dissolvable thread. Tori then patched him up and guided his trembling body into her guest room. She wrapped his leg and then forced him to swallow some Lortabs. When she finally laid him down, he instantly drifted away.

At that point, Tori decided she would steal whatever else she needed from her job to help him, and she would care for him until he was better. She threw away his clothes and carried his heavy bags into the guest room with him, threw both bags in the closet and never gave them a second thought. Her only concern was the bloody gun she left in her car. She decided to hide it in her room in her dresser and she would give it back when he was better, as long as he wasn't crazy.

The moment she entered the guest room, she gasped at the sight before her. Her friend Dora was laying in the bed with her mystery man patient, and she was gently cuddled up against his body. She then noticed he was no longer attached to his IV and there were boxes of Chinese food and plates on the dresser.

"What the fuck!" Tori shouted.

Dora's eyes popped open, and she quickly but quietly eased out of the bed.

"What the fuck are you doing?" Tori scolded.

Dora looked embarrassed when she answered. "He woke up last night."

"How long was he up?" Tori questioned.

"All night. I made sure he ate and then he eventually went back to sleep, but he's fully conscious now."

"Well, how the fuck do you explain being all cuddled up in the bed with this man?" Tori questioned in a firm but low voice. "Just last night you were acting like being here was a problem. You sure seemed pretty comfortable a few seconds ago."

Dora looked embarrassed again, but truthfully answered, "I don't know. Once we ordered the food, we got comfortable and started talking and turned out to be like, extremely cool. I think I like him."

"You think you like him? Dora, you don't even know him!"

"I know, I know, but his spirit seems really alluring and his personality is amazing. You know he is."

"I don't even know him!"

"If you don't know him then what the fuck is he doing here?"

Tori became silent. "I told you I would explain it all today."

"Well, maybe you can explain it later. I'm tired and I'm going home. It's too early for all your mysterious bullshit!" Dora snapped. She then pranced into the kitchen, grabbed her purse off the counter and hustled out of the house.

When Tori turned around to look at the sleeping mystery man, she flinched and blurted out, "Shit! You scared me!"

"My bad," I calmly replied.

She kept her eyes on me and didn't say a word.

Once again, I was blown away by the natural beauty of the woman standing before me.

Déjà vu.

She had on a light gray silk nightgown that hugged her body like a glove. The nightgown stopped mid-thigh and the thin straps hung low on her shoulders. Her skin was dark brown, and she was shaped like a Coke bottle. Her lips were pink, and her eyes were light brown. She had thick eyebrows, but they were sexy. Her breasts were smaller than Dora's, but her thighs and hips were much larger. They also stood about the same height. Her natural hair hung a little past her shoulders. She was staring at me intensely.

"Thank you," I sincerely said.

"I think you owe me much more than a simple thank you," she snapped.

"You're right, I owe you my life and I promise, I'll have a blessing for you."

"Yeah, that sounds nice and all, but how about an apology and an explanation! You forced me into my car at gunpoint!"

I rotated my arm in a circle and said, "Please relax. Getting angry and shouting ain't gone get us nowhere, I do owe you an apology though and I'm sorry. I know the situation may have been scary for you at the time, but I really didn't mean no harm. I just needed help and"

"Then you should've taken your ass inside the hospital and gotten the help you needed! How could you—"

"Listen!" I firmly cut her off. "Lower your tone. I come in peace and I'm beyond thankful for the help you provided me, but if all you gonna do is scream and shit, then I'm out of here."

I swung my legs to the floor and looked around the room.

"And where the hell do you think you're going?" Tori asked in a more manageable tone.

"Where the road takes me. Somewhere where the women don't scream at me." I smirked.

Tori looked at me and probably couldn't believe how arrogant I was being. She was probably thinking I should be showing her more respect. But then again, I really wasn't being disrespectful. I was just very arrogant.

"I really do need to get going though, I wanted to leave when I woke up last night, but your homegirl convinced me to stay until you got here. Now that you're here, I'm ready to go."
I stood up and made sure to lean all of my weight on my right side.

Tori noticed my movements and asked, "Are you in pain?"

"Definitely sore all over, but I think the worst is over."

"I think you should at least stay for a few more days and let me clean your wounds again. You still have a lot of healing to do. Let me at least change your patches and give you some pain medication."

I considered her offer and decided, why not? I've been here all of this time anyway. A few more days wouldn't hurt me. At least that'll give me some time to seriously think about my next move. I got to move smart right now."

"Alright, I'll sit tight," I concluded.

"Good, you should take one of these for now." Tori reached inside the dresser next to me and removed a pill bottle. She popped out two pills and handed them to me.

"Lortabs," she explained. "Helps the pain."

I took the pills and washed them down with one of the water bottles on the dresser from last night.

“So, what's up with my explanation?” Tori asked me.

“What do you wanna know?”

“What’s your name?”

“Wizz”

“Okay, Wizz, what the hell happened to you?”

“Somebody shot me and then I ended up in a car accident,” I simply explained.

“Well, that doesn’t tell me much.”

“It tells you everything you really need to know. That's what happened, the details ain't really that important.” I was very nonchalant, even though the other details were not only very important, but they were also unimaginable.

“Did you do something wrong?”

“Depends on how you look at it. Technically, I didn't, if you consider the original circumstances that led up to the event of me being shot. Or, you could say that my actions along the way were still wrong, which means I did something wrong.”

“Okay, I can see the logic in that. So—”

“Let me ask you a couple questions,” I interrupted her.

“Umm, okay.”

“Why did you help me?”

“Well, honestly, I brought you here against my better judgment and then once you were here, I thought, what if this was my brother?”

“You got a brother?”

“Yeah, he's nineteen and he’s into the whole street life thing.”

“How old are you?”

“Twenty-nine.”

Grown and sexy.

“Did you call the police?”

“No, I didn’t. But I did watch the news to see if there was anything about a shooting and I didn’t see anything in the area.”

“This shit right here should have definitely made the news, but then again, it may have gotten covered up.”

"A cover up?" Tori laughed. "Alright, James Bond."

I smiled. "You'd be surprised. Aye, where we at though?"

"We're at my house."

"Yeah, I go that part, where do you live?"

"My neighborhood ain't got no entrance title, but we're down the street from Mountain Park Apartments off Custer Avenue."

"Mountain Park? Where the fuck is that? What city are we in?"

"East Atlanta."

"Atlanta! What the fuck?" I stared at him with amazement and then it hit me. Bo T must've driven me all the way to a hospital in Atlanta.

Damn!

"Is that a surprise to you?"

"Hell yeah!"

"Where did you expect to be?"

"Shit, I don't know, just didn't expect Atlanta."

"Where are you from?"

"I think that's enough questions for now…One more thing though, thank you for securing my property."

"What property? I threw your clothes away and the money you had in your pockets was covered in blood. There was no way you could've been able to use it, so I threw it all away, I'm sorry."

"I'm talking about my bags."

"Oh! I forgot about those honestly. I've been so caught up in keeping you healthy, I totally forgot. I put them in the closet and forgot about them."

"Well, thank you, that's way more important than everything right now."

"What's in them?"

I looked at her like she was crazy. "Quit playing."

"Playing how?" she sincerely questioned.

Is it possible she never looked in my shit?

"Didn't you look inside?" I quizzed.

"No. I told you, on the first night, I put them in the closet and then I forgot about them."

I stared into her eyes, and she seemed to be telling the truth.

Damn! She played.

I wonder if it would change the situation if she knew I was sitting on a gold mine.

"Alright, well, thanks."

"What's in the bags?" she questioned.

"Just the personal items I've been traveling with."

That wasn't a lie. It wasn't a straight answer, but it definitely wasn't a lie.

"Oh okay, I figured that." she innocently accepted it.

"Where's my gun?"

"In my room." She looked fearful. "Do you need it?"

"Damn right! I need it like right now!"

"Please, don't do anything crazy!"

"I told you, I owe you my life. I promise, you in good hands. I know we had a crazy introduction, but believe me, around me you're safe."

My words must have held some type of weight because she didn't hesitate to leave the room and return with my Glock 17. I checked the clip and made sure it was full. Seventeen rounds ain't bad, but after remembering the story Bo-T told me after the crash, I couldn't help but think I was going to need a lot more than seventeen bullets.

"Do you have clothes to wear?" she asked and looked down on me.

I was sitting on the edge of the bed in some boxers that weren't mine and Lord knows how long I'd been wearing them?"

"Uhh, naw! Who boxers I got on?"

"My brother's. It was all I could find at the time."

"How did I get in them?"

Tori blushed and replied, "I'm a doctor. I've seen naked people many times. I put you in them."

"Just asking." I smiled. "I ain't got nothing to be ashamed of."

She ignored my comments and asked, "Don't you have clothes in your bags?"

"Nawl, unfortunately, I don't."

"Well, I'm kind of tired right now, but maybe later I'll go out to Walmart or something and get you something simple to wear for the time being."

"Go ahead and rest up. We'll worry about the clothes later. I'm hungry though."

"I got some cereal in the kitchen, that's about it. I need to go food shopping."

"What kind of cereal do you have?"

"Cheerios."

"Cheerios?"

"Yeah, Negro, Cheerios. What's wrong with that?"

"Who the fuck eats Cheerios?" I laughed. "My mama eats Cheerios, not me. What else you got?"

"Well, yo mama got good taste. And that's all I got."

"You got the app on your phone to order food?"

"Yeah, but I ain't got paid yet. I can't afford to get you some food, go food shopping, and buy you some reasonable clothes later."

"You're talking about buying me clothes like I'm moving in or something."

"I'm just tryna help. All I was going to get is some underwear and some shirts, maybe a pair of shorts."

"Well, I appreciate the courtesy, but I'll worry about the payment. Do you have the app or not?"

"Yeah, of course."

"Alright, give me your phone and go to sleep. I'll be fine."

"Please don't do nothing stupid."

"What did I tell you? You're in good hands like Allstate. Just chill."

Tori left the room for the second time and returned with her phone. She tossed it to me and said, "Enjoy."

When Tori went back to her room, she wasn't sure what to think. Her job here was done. The mystery man was up and apparently fine.

So, why was she still helping him?

He wanted to leave.

Shouldn't she just let him go?

She did want to make sure he healed properly before he left but there was something else. Dora said he had a good spirit and now that he was up, she could feel it.

There was still a lot she wanted to know about Wizz and something about him was very intriguing. She still didn’t know him at all. So, what was it?

Was it the tattoos that completely covered his light-skinned body? Or was it his mouth full of glistening gold teeth? Was it his bright hazel eyes?

So what, he was sexy. This man could be trouble.

Well, she had a few more days to figure it out.

Chapter 3

After I stuffed my face with the four breakfast sandwiches I had ordered from Waffle House, I went back to the room I've been sleeping in and pulled one of my bags out of the closet. I needed to pull out enough money to buy me some clothes later on. This chick talking about she gone get me some shorts and some shirts from Walmart.

Ha! That's funny.

I guess it's the thought that counts, but she most definitely had me fucked up!

I ain't never been in Atlanta before, and it ain't no way in hell I was going to be caught walking around a city like Atlanta, in an outfit from Walmart. I also wanted to surprise Tori and allow her to do some shopping for herself. After that, I'd take her food shopping and that would conclude our travels for the day.

I pulled out what I felt was a reasonable amount, nothing major, not for me anyway. Didn't even put a dent in my baby. I stacked the money on the dresser and walked back into the living room. There was a clock on the wall that let me know it was a little after nine in the morning.

Where did Tori sleep?

There was only three bedrooms in the house. I slept in one and there's another across the hall from mine. I'm sure that wasn't her room, so her room had to be somewhere towards the back of the house.

I walked beyond the kitchen, through a den, and found another room. The door was slightly cracked, so I simply opened it wider and looked inside. Tori must have sensed my presence because she rolled over in bed and looked straight at me.

I stepped into the room, and she quickly sat up in her bed. Her movements gave me the impression that she was scared. I guess she had that right, but I told her she was straight.

I stopped halfway towards her bed and raised my hands. "I ain't mean to wake you up. I was just walking around the house and wondered where your room was."

She looked at me for a long moment then said, "Did you eat?"

"Yeah, I ended up ordering some Waffle House."

She looked at the clock on her dresser and said, "Well, I guess I'll get up now and we can get this day started."

"You can go back to sleep if you want. I ain't in no rush and you only slept for about two hours."

"I'm good. I'mma just take a quick shower and then I'll be ready," she spoke while easing her way out of her bed.

Her nightgown rode up on her wide hips and I caught a glimpse of her bright pink panties.

"How am I supposed to go out like this?" I questioned and gestured at the fact that I was still only wearing boxers.

She walked over to her dresser and opened the bottom drawer. Her ass cheeks spread as she bent over and I immediately thought, maybe this is a great spot to stay for the time being.

She stood back up and handed me some black sweatpants, some socks and a black tank top. She then glided across the floor to the closet and tossed me a pair of black Nike slides. The whole time she's walking around, all I kept thinking was, damn that ass fat! It wasn't fat like the woman I left behind in Florida, but it was most definitely fat.

"That should get you there and back," she stated and then headed into her bathroom.

She shut the door and not long after I heard the shower water running. I left the room and headed back to mine. I stuffed the neat stacks of money where I could fit them. One stack in each of two pockets and one stack in both of my socks. I rolled the sweatpants over my ankles and since the sweats fit me loosely, you couldn't tell I was cuffing.

I used the toiletries in the bathroom to clean up and then looked in the mirror. I definitely needed to get my hair cut and cleaned up. I strolled back to the living room and waited for Tori.

Before long, we were climbing into her Benz and driving away.

"Alright, so where do you wanna go?" Tori asked me. "There's a Walmart down the street."

"Thanks, but no thanks. I think I wanna go to a barber shop first and then I wanna go shopping at Lenox."

"Lenox? That's ridiculous. You'll come out way cheaper if you go somewhere simple. We could go to Marshalls or—"

"This isn't a debate. Barber shop, then Lenox. We gone shop together. I wanna get a few outfits for myself and then a few things for you as well."

"For me? I mean, that's very thoughtful, but I'm fine. I don't ne—"

"Not a debate, Tori. I told you, you're in good hands. Nothing major, just a few outfits and shoes for me and whatever you can manage with what I got for you…For now."

Tori looked unsure while turning into a plaza with a barber shop and then said, "Okay, well how much are you trying to spend at the mall?"

"Twenty on me, twenty on you," I nonchalantly answered.

"Twenty? Your damn hair cut going to cost you twenty dollars alone. How the hell you gonna go shopping with twenty—"

"Twenty dollars?" I shook my head with a frown. "I feel disrespected."

"How?"

"Twenty, means twenty thousand! What type of niggas you been dealing with?"

"Twenty thousand!" Tori shrieked.

"Uhh…yeah," I calmly stated and then exited the car.

I think Tori took me for a joke at first, but hours later, we were pulling back into her driveway with lots of designer clothes and lots of food for her refrigerator.

We put the food up first and then we retrieved our clothes. I tossed all of my bags on the floor and then walked over to Tori's room.

"You good?" I asked while stepping through the door.

"Am I good? I've never spent money like that in my life! Not on clothes anyway. And then you wouldn't even let me spend it wisely! Twenty thousand dollars and all I got to show for it is three outfits, four dresses, a purse and seven heels!"

"Yeah, I don't know what type of shit you've been buying, but I couldn't just sit back and watch you buy all that cheap ass bullshit. Naw, not on my watch." I smiled.

"This is ridiculous!" she joyfully shouted.

"Once again, you're in good hands, I'm glad you're happy. You have a very beautiful smile and I'm proud to be the one that caused it."

Tori blushed and I could tell she was really feeling me. She had been trying to act cool all day, but I could feel her eyes on me whenever she thought I wasn't looking, and the smile on her face right now was impossible to hide. I'll play her little game though. No pressure.

Really found it hard to believe she stayed here by herself, and she didn't have a nigga. A beautiful black woman that was a certified doctor and surgeon. Independent, with her own house, own car and own money and above all, black and beautiful!

What the fuck wrong with these niggas out here?

But her excuse was that she had done eight years in college and was so caught up in school and solidifying her career, that she never made time for a man.

Well, lucky me! But what about Dora?

Me and Dora clicked off the dribble and I could tell she was openly feeling me. Every bitch I come in contact with is feeling me though. That ain't nothing new. But in a situation like this, I knew I couldn't have both of them.

Or could I?

Man, I just met these hoes. Fuck it. I'll just let shit play out.

"Well, alright. I'm finna kick back and relax a little bit. I ain't got my mind right in a minute, so that's on my immediate to-do list. You mind me smoking in the house?" I spoke.

"Nah, you good. Make yourself comfortable," she replied while emptying her new bags.

"Alright, I'll be in the living room."

"I'll join you in a few after I put these clothes up."

"Kool," I stated while leaving the room.

Back in the room, I pulled out my bag with my weed in it and removed a heavily-compressed-pound bag. I ripped it open, and the familiar aroma was so pleasant I nearly fainted. I love that hoe, Mary Jane.

I grabbed two blunts out of one of my shopping bags and carried the whole pound into the living room. I rolled up, fired up, and let the medication take effect. Cloud nine was a wonderful place.

I suddenly heard a key rattling in the front door and that threw me off.

Did Tori step outside?

I quickly turned toward the door and watched a young nigga stumble inside the house with a blue book bag and begin fumbling with the locks on the door. His hands were shaking so badly, it took him nearly a whole minute to simply lock the damn door.

Or was I so high, he was moving in slow motion?

The young nigga then turned, and we locked eyes. He froze like a deer caught in headlights.

"Who the fuck is you?" the jitterbug blurted with plenty of animosity.

In my head I was asking him the same question, but before I could open my mouth to speak, Tori stepped into the living room.

"Aye sis, who the fuck this nigga is?" the youngin asked Tori.

"Vonn, what the hell are you doing over here? What I told you about popping up in my house unexpectedly?" Tori questioned

"My bad, sis. I just got caught in a sticky situation and I need somewhere to lay low for a minute," Vonn answered.

"Nigga, do this look like a hide out?" Tori rolled her eyes. "Don't be bringing your bullshit and problems to my home."

I sat quietly and continued puffing on my blunt while carefully watching the interaction between Tori and this young nigga, who at this point, I'm assuming is her little brother.

"Just let me hang out for the night and I'll be out yo way by tomorrow. I just wanna make sure the coast is clear before I step back out yo way by tomorrow," Vonn pleaded.

"What the hell you done did now?" Tori questioned.

Before Vonn answered her question, he glanced in my direction. “I’d rather not say.”

Tori sat down next to me on the couch and said to Vonn, “Well, alright. The guest room ain’t available, but you can sleep out here on the couch.”

Vonn flopped down on the loveseat across from us and asked, “Who in the guest room?”

“My guest,” Tori replied and nodded towards me.

“And who the fuck is he?” Vonn asked with all the previous hostility returned to his voice.

“This is my friend, Wizz. And you need to stop being rude.” Tori then looked at me and said, “Wizz, this is my annoying little brother, Vonn.”

I blew out a cloud of smoke and finally spoke. “What up, jit?”

Vonn looked me up and down and examined my features. I had street nigga written all over me and I guess this was a new sight in his sister’s house.

He brushed me off and looked at his sister. “This yo boyfriend or something?”

I disregarded the minor disrespect for two reasons. One, I wasn’t in no condition to be trying to ball this nigga up. Two, I done been a young ass nigga before, so I know how it is.

“This is my friend, like I told you,” Tori replied.

He looked at me again and took notice of the large patch on my shoulder. “What happened to your shoulder?”

I blew out another cloud of smoke. “Got shot by the police.”

“Damn!” Vonn blurted

Tori looked at me and raised one eyebrow. “You ain’t tell me the police did this to you.”

I shrugged. “Didn't know it mattered.”

I attempted to pass Tori the blunt, but she denied the offer.

“I don't smoke,” she stated firmly.

I shrugged. “More for me.”

I took three more pulls and put the remaining piece of the blunt down on the cup holder I was using as an ashtray. There wasn't much remaining. I looked at Vonn and his hands were still slightly trembling.

"You straight, lil bra?" I questioned.

"Yeah, I'm good," Vonn spoke with a bravado that didn't match his movements.

"Looks like you need to calm your nerves. Roll up!" I started and tossed him my other blunt.

He reached in his pocket and pulled out a nickel bag of weed. I shook my head.

I remember those days.

I lifted the pound of weed I had resting on the floor between my legs and tossed it on the table between us. A few nuggets fell out of the bag and rolled across the table. His eyes grew wide, but he didn't speak.

"You might as well put that shit back in yo pocket, lil bra. Whenever you're around me, I got you, you good. Especially since this your sister. Roll up some of that good."

Tori looked at me and smiled. The pound of weed didn't even seem to surprise her. I'm sure she realized by now I wasn't no petty nigga.

"That's real, bet that up," Von stated and began the rolling process.

Once he got the blunt rolled and lit, he took a few pulls and seemed to instantly relax. He tried to pass me the blunt after his fourth hit, but I shook my head.

"Hang out, jit. I'm good," I said.

"I be hearing niggas say that shit in rap songs, but I ain't never had none," Vonn admitted.

I could see and sense Vonn was beginning to loosen up and I couldn't help but remember how it was for me when I was his age.

The three of us hung out in the living room for another couple of hours, and eventually ordered some pizza. After we ate, Tori decided to take it in and get some rest. I told her to be ready to do a little more shopping in the morning because there were a few more things I wanted to get. The smile on her face let me know she couldn't wait and then she was gone. That left me and Vonn.

"So, what's good, lil bra?"

"Whatever you wanna do," Vonn replied.

I could tell Vonn was beginning to look up to me. I consciously debated taking jit under my wing and molding him into a young rich nigga, but I still wasn't sure how long I'd be here. After I grabbed another blunt from out of the room, I tossed it to Vonn and decided to see what type of shit he was into.

"So, what happened to you tonight?" I questioned.

While busting open the blunt, he replied, "Me and one of my dawgs robbed this nigga that was tryna serve us, but some lady fucked around and peeped the lick and called the police. Me and my dawg split up and took off on foot. I ain't have no wheels so I ran the whole way here."

"What y'all hit for?" I was curious.

Vonn emptied the blue backpack on the table and two ounces of molly, a ball of coke, and a bottle of pills tumbled out. Vonn then looked at me and smiled. I shook my head and frowned.

I definitely remember those days.

"Looks like maybe a two-thousand-dollar lick." I guessed. "What's the split?"

"Fifty-fifty with my dawg."

"So, you come out with somewhere around a thousand." I shook my head. "And you say a lady peeped the play? That's a witness! A witness that can and will take the stand on you if you fuck around and get caught. And if that were to happen, how could you afford a lawyer with only a grand?"

"Ain't nobody getting caught. A grand is a big come up," Vonn stated proudly.

"I admire your heart and your go-get- 'em attitude. I've been there before, but I've also been to prison. Have you been to prison yet?"

"Prison? Hell naw! I don't even think like that. I—"

"Keep committing first degree felonies for a stack and you'll make it there. I used to have that same mentality until one day, reality hit. It's gonna be your mistake that sends you to prison. It's gonna be somebody else's mistake that you have to pay for. Then once you realize the thousand you risked it all for, the thousand you won't have by your first court dates, won't save you, you gone feel real stupid!"

Vonn just stared at me and fired up. He rolled a blunt, took a puff and seemed to be considering my words. He was listening. I like that.

"Listen to me, lil bra. I have been there and done that. I'm speaking from experience. I ain't gone never tell you no bullshit. I'm just giving you reality and things to consider. Everybody starts from the bottom, but you gotta be smart if your goal is the top. Right now, I'm a long way from the bottom. Listen to me and ride with me, lil bra. I'll make you a beast out here in the streets of Atlanta. Once you start getting real money, your whole mindset will change. What are you gonna do?"

I accepted the blunt from Vonn and watched the wheels turning in his head. I didn't even show him anything yet, but he could tell I was on some boss shit.

"I'm fucking with you, big bra…Give me the game," Vonn decided.

Chapter 4

Another three weeks had gone by, and I was finally feeling as good as new. I was pretty much my regular self, but I had a slight permanent limp in my walk due to some type of minor nerve damage. That's how Tori explained it.

At this point I had spent all of my time with either Tori, her little brother Vonn, or by myself. Tori was definitely digging me, but she stuck to her guns and politely refused all of my advances. That really only made me want her more thought. I hadn't seen Dora again and that was cool with me.

Somewhere along the line Tori ended up asking me what had happened to me again and wanted to know how I ended up at the hospital the way I was. I ended up telling her I was riding with my brother, and he had a warrant for some serious shit. I then explained how we were riding and when the police got behind us, my brother mashed the gas.

I told her during the high-speed chase, the police tried to shoot out our tires and somehow, I ended up getting shot. Then we crashed. I then lied a little and said that the officer chasing us had also crashed. I then lied a little and said the officer chasing us had also crashed and at that point, we were able to get away.

I told her I passed out in the car and woke up in front of the hospital. We came from Florida, so I had no idea that I was in Georgia. My brother didn't want to risk being caught so he dropped me off at the hospital and took off.

She could tell I was omitting a lot of details, but she still accepted my story. She told me on a regular day there was no way she would harbor a fugitive, but she was making an exception at the moment because I was—in her words—a cutie.

Vonn was turning out to be a cool lil nigga with a lot of potential. He had nine homeboys and they called themselves *The Nino Boys*. They all had friends and their girls called themself *The Nina Girls.* I found that funny, but to my surprise, they actually had a name in the city. Nothing major but they were basically known for being bad asses. That was the best way to put it.

I would hang with Vonn whenever Tori was at work and that's when I'd school him. Out of his nine homies, he was the second oldest and the youngest was seventeen. I ended up giving him two kilos of coke and I told him to bring me back thirty-six stacks.

His eyes lit up like they were full of fireflies and he damn near fainted. He wouldn't believe he was being blessed with that kind of opportunity, he had never even seen a brick before and now he was being granted two of them for an unbelievable price. That put him on a whole new magnitude.

I did that for two reasons. One, I ain't have the time more patience to be sitting around selling no dope. That was a headache I didn't want. So, why not front a couple to lil bra and give him a chance to move it for me? I had twelve of them to play with.

My second reason was that I wanted to start boosting Vonn's ego. I needed him to start having that bossed-up rich nigga mentality. By dropping the work off on him, it would not only boost his ego, but it would also solidify his position as the head honcho amongst his peers

The Nino Boys and Nina Girls would look up to him as their leader. He would be the plug and he would decide who ate and what positions everybody would play. A structure would be formed, and it was all in his hands. And since he was in my hands, that meant I'd be inheriting a group of souljas. That could be useful.

At the same time, his new baller status would quickly spread through the streets like wildfire and that would open up new opportunities to do what I do best. Rob niggas! I told him to leave all the petty licks for the petty niggas and to reel in the big fish. Once he had a big fish on the hook, I'd step in and check the nigga resume.

I made it very clear I never wanted my location, or my identity revealed to nobody. Not even his closet comrades. I was his new plug and never questioned.

Now, here I was sitting at the house bored and by myself. Tori had just left for work about an hour ago and now that I was feeling fully operable, I was horny! Even though Tori wasn't tryna give me no pussy, she damn sure wasn't tryna let me leave her shoes. Every time I brought up the subject of going on about my business, he would come up with a reason why I should stay. At this point, I actually felt like I had the perfect set-up, and I had no intentions on leaving. I just like to mess with her head sometimes.

All in all, I ain't mind playing her game for now, but I definitely needed to step up and make something happen. A nigga needed to see a woman's ass and titties. I grabbed the house phone and called Vonn.

"What's good?" Vonn answered.

"What's up, lil bra, where are you at?"

"Hangin in the hood with my Ninos."

"What y'all up to?"

"Just tryna get this money, big bra."

"I can dig it. What have you got planned for tonight?"

"Uhh, nothing that I can think of. What's good?"

"I'm tryna hang out and hit a hot spot tonight. I want you to ride with me."

"Alright, shit, where are you tryna go?"

"I wanna see what's up with Magic City."

"Magic City? Damn. I ain't gone lie, big bra, I ain't never been to no strip club before."

"Nigga, you ain't never what? You stay in Atlanta and you ain't never been to a strip club?" Even though Vonn couldn't see me I was shaking my head. "I be forgetting you a young ass nigga. Your broke ass can't afford to hang with no strippers."

"You got me fucked up! I ain't broke!"

"Well, put yo money where yo mouth is, jit! Get ya shit together and meet me at the house." I hung up before he could respond.

I know Vonn ain't got enough money to really hang out like me right now, but I like to fuck with his head. I planned on bringing more than enough money for the both of us. Tonight, I planned on having fun.

***

It was a little after 10:00 p.m. when Vonn called the house to let me know he was outside. I was looking like my usual self as I stepped out of the house and locked the door. I had on an outfit and enough jewelry to light up a stadium.

I hopped into the passenger seat and leaned the seat back. Lil bra was riding in a 2020 dark blue Infiniti.

"Who car this is?" I asked while lighting the blunt I had already rolled.

"This my dawg shit. He wanted to ride with us to the club. He went home to get ready, so I told him to let me scoop you up while he was getting right since I know you don't want nobody to know where you are. We gone go back to his spot, pick him up, then head out," Vonn explained.

"Sounds like a plan," I stated while passing Vonn the blunt.

"How much money you rolling with? Strippers like rich niggas. Don't go in there cramping my style, jit," I joked.

"I got eleven hundred for them hoes," Vonn boasted.

"Eleven hundred? Maaaannn, take me back home, jit. You gone fuck around and make me look bad," I laughed. I reached in my pocket and tossed Vonn a stack of hundreds I had brought for his enjoyment. "This is your first time in a strip club, and it's Magic City at that. Hang out, lil bra. I want you to blow all that tonight."

Vonn eyes the stack of hundreds in his lap and smiles harder. "You ain't gotta tell me twice! We finna be lit!"

"Damn right! Every time we party, we gone party like rock stars, nigga!"

We eventually scooped up his homeboy and then headed for the club. So far, I had met four of his homies and the young nigga now riding with us wasn't one of them. Vonn kept the music blasting until we reached the club and when we finally made it, I turned the car light on and checked myself in the rearview mirror.

As soon as the music stopped and the light came on, Vonn's homeboy blurted out, "Oh shit! That's Tyga!"

Me and Vonn both started laughing.

I looked back and greeted the young nigga. "What's up, youngin? Who are you be?"

"They call me FN…That stands for Fat Nino." He had the perfect name. He was a little fat nigga, but he had sauce though. He had short dreads and a baby face. The lump in his pocket let me know he was getting the money.

After introducing myself to FN, we headed for the club. I felt kind of funny hanging out with these young ass niggas, but I didn't look out of place. After doing them nine years in the joint, I still looked young as fuck my damn self. They say prison preserves you. At twenty-eight, I could easily pass for twenty-two or twenty-three, probably even younger.

Vonn and FN started walking toward the line and I immediately cussed them niggas out.

"What the fuck y'all doing?" I blurted.

"What do you mean? We are getting in line," Vonn stated like the answer was obvious.

"Nigga, I wouldn't give a fuck if they called it the G-O-D line! A line is a line and we ain't standing in it," I blurted while heading towards the door.

Vonn and FN quickly followed suit and got behind me. I approached the two bouncers at the door and let my appearance and my money do all the talking. Without ever speaking, I reached into one of my pockets and pulled out a ten-thousand-dollar stack of hundreds and slowly peeled off a grand. I put the rest back in my pocket.

I handed five hundred to the bouncer on the night and the other five hundred to the bouncer on the left. I pointed at Vonn and FN and then stepped forward. With no hesitation, the bouncer on the left quickly removed the velvet rope from in front of me and let the three of us pass. A slim, brown-skinned woman strapped a blue band around our wrists and then went inside the club.

The moment we entered, the music was blaring, and The City Girls were screaming through the speakers. I looked around and I was very delighted with the sight around me. Definitely, what I wanted to see. Ass and titties. Lots of it!

I approached the bar with my two youngins and waited for a bartender to approach us, which didn't take long.

Before she could get me, I dropped two bundles of money on the counter and said, "Let me get all ones for this."

I flashed my glistening teeth, and the woman matched my smile.

"How much is this?" she asked me.

"Nineteen bands, but I think my lil brother needs some ones too," I spoke and nodded at Vonn.

Vonn quickly took that as his cue and dropped his stack on the counter next to mine.

"That's another ten right there," I said.

"Twenty-nine thousand? I'll have to take this to the manager, and he will provide the money you've requested," the bartender stated.

"Alright, cool. Let me get two bottles of ACE while I wait."

The bartender quickly fulfilled my order and then disappeared with the money.

"Damn! Y'all doing it like that?" FN blurted to Vonn.

"Rich nigga shit!" Von blurted back.

FN then looked at me with a big ass smile on his fat baby face. I popped one of the bottles and poured the three of us a drink. I then looked around at the bountiful supply of beauties. They should call these places Heaven on Earth!

Moments later, the bartender returned with a clear bag of penalty blocked-dollar bills and sat the bag in front of me on the counter.

"The manager said to enjoy your night," the bar girl spoke.

I casually looked around and saw the strippers eyeballing us. I opened the bag and handed ten blocks of money to Vonn. I then handed four blocks to FN. I lifted the rest of the bag and we headed for the heart of the action.

"Let's hang out!" I shouted over the music.

We made our way towards a stage, while admiring the many shades of ass cheeks clapping around us. The stage we approached had a variety of women on it, but the first beauty that grabbed my attention was a dark-skinned stallion with long braids. Her chocolate booty cheeks were bouncing like basketballs, and she was squatting right in my face.

"Whoa!

I popped the ban on one of my thousand-dollar stacks and split it in two halves. I tossed one half all at once and watched the single bills rain over the chocolate basketballs in front of me. She looked at all the money floating around her and started shaking her ass harder.

There was a light-skinned honey with an unnaturally small waist and bubble butt, doing her thing on all-fours to my right, and I quickly showered her with the other half of my stack.

While popping the band on another stack, I saw another cloud of singles burst into the air. I looked over at Vonn and smiled. His face looked like a kids in a candy store.

A super thick, brown-skinned chick with an ass that moved like Jello suddenly forced me to give her my undivided attention. I pulled up right behind her and clouded her with a full thousand-dollar stack. She smiled and bent over right in my face. She spread her cheeks apart and looked at me between her legs.

Damn!

You already know I hit lil baby with another stack

"Damn, lil mama shaking that asss!" Vonn blurted and pointed at a short, petite, dark-skinned woman who was wearing a curve-hugging, white mini dress.

"Yeah, baby bouncing that ass real nice" FN stated and walked towards her before anyone else could speak.

I watched FN toss a couple hundred on the short woman and by the dirty looks the dancers were giving, I could tell the woman in the white dress wasn't a stripper. Not here anyway.

Two more women appeared next to the short chick, and they appeared to have the same features. Short and black, petite, and wearing a mini dress. I tapped Vonn on the arm and together, we headed over. I quickly examined the two women. One had on red, the other had on blue, other than that they appeared to be on the same scale. I chose the one on the road.

I grabbed the red dress by the hips and whispered in her ear. "What's good, baby, what are you doing in here?"

She looked me up and down and couldn't contain her smile. Bitch probably thought I was a rapper.

"I'm just enjoying a carefree night with the fam," she replied and gestured towards the other two women.

I laid my billion-dollar mac down and eventually found out that her and blue dress were sisters, and white dress was their little cousin. They were just hanging out and enjoying a night of fun, while their boyfriends were out of town handling business.

I asked red dress if she wanted to slide to a hotel with me and she told me buying a room would be pointless since we could all chill at her spot. Her man was out of town so the coast was clear, and she would enjoy my company. I told red telling her money wasn't an issue, but she wasn't tryna hear that shit. She said she would feel more comfortable at home.

Against my better judgment, I decided to roll with her offer.

I hope this bitch ain't tryna set me up.

I told Vonn and FN to wrap it out. We hung out a little longer, thew a little more money, and within the next hour we were following the three women out of the club.

Chapter 5

I hopped out of the car at red dress' house and manneredly staggered into her two-story home. Of course, I had no idea where the fuck I was at. Shit, I was just starting to get a geographical understanding of the area I was living in around Tori's house.

Vonn and FN entered the home with me, and we all took a seat in the living room. The three women ran upstairs and said they would be back down after they freshened up. I kicked my feet up on the coffee table and began rolling up a blunt without a care in the world.

About halfway through the blunt, the three women came gliding back down the stairs and they all appeared to have exchanged their red, white and blue mini dresses for red, white and blue lingerie.

Damn!

Red lingerie had a fat, fluffy ass pussy! If it weren't for the fact that her lingerie was slightly transparent, I would've thought she was either wearing a pad, or in desperate need of a shave.

Yikes!

My new friend for the moment slowly eased her way onto my lap and the other women did the same with Vonn and FN. I don't know about everybody else, but as for me, I was ready to get the party started. I smoothly moved my hand between her legs and began gently rubbing on her soft dark lips. She parted her thighs to give me more room, so I swiftly slipped her red panties to the side.

I licked two of my fingers and slowly teased them inside of her. She leaned into me and moaned into my ear.

Bam! Bam! Bam!

"Oh shit!" one of the other girls blurted.

My play date quickly jumped off of my lap and her once lustful face appeared to lose all of its life. She looked terrified.

Bam! Bam! Bam!

"Open this door, you trick ass bitch!" somebody shouted from the other side of the front door. That somebody was definitely a male by the way.

"I thought you said Kenny was out of town!" Blue lingerie blurted to red lingerie.

"He's supposed to be!" Red lingerie blurted back.

"Bitch, don't make me kick this bitch down!" the man shouted from outside.

"Y'all go upstairs!" Red lingerie barely blurted in our direction.

"What the fuck I look like? A teenager? Bitch, I ain't hiding in no muhfucking closet!" I quickly blurted back. I stood up, fixed my pants and adjusted my cannon.

"Please just go upstairs! Y'all ain't gotta hide, just go upstairs for a moment so I can make it seem like we were just chilling and make him leave," Red lingerie pleaded.

Vonn and FN looked at me as if every little thing we did was always up to me, so I decided once again against my better judgment to give this bitch a chance to pull a fast one. I still wanted the pussy. We quickly slipped up the stairs and waited at the IHOP around a corner. I felt like I was back in fucking high school.

BAM! BAM! BAM! BAM!

"Nigga, why the fuck is you banging on my damn door at two in the fucking morning!" Red lingerie shouted while swinging the door open.

Her boyfriend quickly pushed her in the face and stepped inside of the house. He looked around and only saw the two other women chilling on the couch curled up under some covers.

"Where the fuck them niggas at?" the nigga shouted.

"Kenny, what the fuck is you talki—"

Whap!

Kenny slapped red lingerie right across her mouth and shouted, "Bitch, don't play with me! My homeboy told me he seen your triflin ass at Magic City shaking yo ass and you left with three niggas! You and them two trick bitches on the couch!"

"Kenny, I swear, I—"

Whap!

Blue lingerie leaped from the couch and shouted, "Nigga, you done lost your damn mind if you think you gone use my sister as a punching bag! I'm about to all the police on yo stupid ass!"

"Fuck you too, bitch! Where the fuck them niggas at?" Kenny shouted and began walking around the first floor of the house.

I pulled my Glock 17 out and cocked it back. "Fuck this shit, let's just walk out," I instructed my youngins.

We began quickly descending the steps and right before we could make it to the bottom, we were met by a roadblock. Kenny turned out to be a big, muscle-bound black nigga, with muscles in places that were unnecessary. He looked like a bull about to charge and just as the thought crossed my mind, he made a huge mistake. He charged.

I nonchalantly lifted my Glock and double-tapped the trigger

Boom! Boom!

The in-house gunshots were deafening. Kenny instantly dropped to the floor, and we quickly hopped over his body.

"Oh my God, no!" Red lingerie shouted and rushed over to her man.

Kenny was already dead.

"Kenny! You killed him! You—"

Boom!

I put a bullet straight into the back of her dome and then quickly turned towards the other two women. White lingerie had her hands over her mouth frozen with fear and blue lingerie had just gotten off the phone with the police. She was also frozen in fear. I had heard her whole phone conversation though and she hasn't reported a homicide. She was already off of the phone by the time my gum started barking. She simply reported some domestic violence type shit.

Oh well…don't matter…no witnesses!

Boom!

Down went blue lingerie. White lingerie attempted to scramble towards the front door.

Boom! Boom!

Down went white lingerie.

I gestured to Vonn and FN that it was now clearly time to go, and we departed the house. Since I was the one driving when we followed the women home, I had the keys to the rental. I quickly tossed them to Vonn and headed for the passenger seat.

"I'm drunk as fuck! I'm liable to wreck this bitch," Vonn slurred and then tossed the keys to FN.

FN jumped in the driver's seat, Vonn jumped in the back, I jumped in the passenger, and then the car came to life. I definitely didn't like the set up, but I couldn't drive because I ain't know where the fuck we was at!

As soon as we backed out of the driveway, I noticed a police cruiser casually making its way down the block in our direction.

"Don't panic!" I blurted to FN in a voice that sounded like I was about to panic. "Just cruise by him," I instructed.

We headed up the residential street at a normal pace and as we drove past the cruiser, the cop driving shone a bright light into our car. The blinding white light seemed to smack me dead in the face and I threw my hands up to cover the beam. The light quickly faded, and we washed by.

I looked back through the rear window and noticed the cruiser pull into the same driveway we just pulled out of.

Ain't no way in hell he didn't see us just leave the same house.

I watched the cop step out of the cruiser and he appeared to be tall and white.

"Alright, pick up the pace a little bit. Get us to the end of the street and turn off," I coached FN.

The rental sped up and as we made it to the end of the road, I took another glance behind me. The tall white cop was sprinting back to his cruiser and talking into the radio that was attached to his shoulder.

"Alright, punch it!" he ordered.

FN mashed the gas as we were turning and caused the tires to screech as we sped away. Two more turns and we were at the front of the neighborhood. We shot out the entrance like a bat out of hell and barely avoided a collision with a sports car.

"Take us to Vonn's house!" I blurted.

Vonn had his own apartment with his girlfriend Alina. They called her N/A. To the women she brushed shoulders with, N/A stood for Nina Alina, and to any nigga that approached her, it stood for not available.

We zoomed through a yellow light right before it turned red and then swerved on a side street. We turned down a back street and tail whipped around an old building. Out of nowhere, red and blue lights began flashing behind us.

Shit!

FN punched the gas and squeezed us into an alley.

"Slide through the projects and bust out the back!" Vonn blurted to FN with the slur from earlier no longer in his voice.

As soon as we made it to the end of the alley, we kept a Nascar fast pace and made a hard right on two wheels.

Crash!

We got blindsided by a truck! The truck knocked us back on all four wheels and sent us skidding across the street. FN had no control over the car at this point and everything was a blur as it happened with lightning speed. We screeched over a curb and came to a sudden halt as we crashed into a concrete light pole.

Smoke rose from the car and the tires continued to screech and burn rubber even though we were no longer moving. I felt kind of dizzy, but my senses were on high alert. I looked over at FN and he was slumped over the steering wheel with blood running down his face and his foot was stuck on the gas. I quickly shook him, but his eyes remained closed.

I looked back at Vonn, and he was staring straight at me with wide eyes,

"Skram nigga, skram!" I shouted and attempted to get out of the car.

The door was jammed shut, so I kicked out the window and climbed out. Vonn helped me up and we dashed away on foot. We quickly bent a corner and kept running like track star until we entered an apartment complex. Our adrenaline was clearly sky high because we didn't even attempt to slow down until we jumped over a fence get in the back of the complex. We jogged through two more neighborhoods and eventually stopped in front of a beat-up white house in a low budget neighborhood.

Vonn whipped his phone out and made a quick call to somebody.

"Are you at home?" Vonn huffed into the phone. "Open the door, bra! Hurry up!" he shouted after receiving his answer. He hung up and placed the phone back in his pocket.

One minute later, the door swung open and one of the Nino Boys I had already met, TNT (Trap Nino Trap) stood in the doorway. We quickly brushed by him and entered the house.

"What's good?" TNT greeted while him and Vonn dabbed each other up.

"Man, bra, shit just got real!" Vonn blurted in a distraught voice.

I sat down on the couch and pulled out a sandwich bag of weed.

"Let me get a blunt, lil bra," I started to TNT.

Vonn joined me on the couch while TNT disappeared down a hallway.

"Don't mention the bodies," I quickly informed Vonn.

Vonn nodded his understanding and then TNT re-entered the living room with a Dutch blunt. I accepted the blunt and began rolling up. Even though I appeared cool, I really needed to calm my unseen nerves.

"Let me and big bra crash here for the night and then we'll slide in the morning," Vonn spoke to TNT,

"I'm cool with that, but what's good though? What got y'all all spooked up? You shaking like a stripper," TNT spoke.

Vonn was nervously shaking like he was the night I met him. I fired up the blunt and passed it to him. I could tell she needed it.

Vonn took the blunt, took a deep pull, and then spoke to TNT.

"Man…bra, we were hanging out with FN and ended up getting caught up in some shit with twelve. FN was driving but he played. We tried to peel on them crackas and ended up wrecking out!"

"Damn, so where is FN at?" TNT questioned.

"Lil bra was knocked out in the car. Me and big bra jumped out after the wreck and took off on foot," Vonn explained and then passed the blunt to TNT.

"Damn, that's some fucked up shit," TNT mumbled. "I hope bra straight."

Vonn pulled his phone out again and made another call.

"Aye bae, aye…I need you to swing by TNT's spot and pick me up in the morning," Vonn spoke. "Alright, just pick me up after you handle that. I ain't going nowhere...Alright…yeah…love you too." He ended his call and leaned back.

Vonn then turned towards me and said, "My girl gone to come get us in the morning after she takes her lil sister to a doctor's appointment. I didn't tell her you were with me, but it's cool. She ain't gone trip."

With that being said, I told TNT to grab us some more blunts and the three of us smoked until we passed out. It had an interestingly unexpected night. It seems like I can't never have any regular fun these days. Nigga tried to get some pussy and ended up catching four bodies! And I still ain't get no pussy!

Damn…

Chapter 6

It was almost one o'clock in the afternoon when Nina Alina showed up at TNT's house. When we got to Vonn's apartment Nina Alina got out and me and Vonn changed our seating arrangement. He was now in the driver's seat, and I was now the passenger. Vonn told his girl he'd be back after he dropped me off and she simply waved as we pulled away.

We stopped at a McDonald's, grabbed a couple burgers, and then Vonn dropped me off at Tori's house. During the ride, he told me FN had a girl named Nina Ross that stayed in some apartments on the west side, so I told him to swing over there after he dropped me off and to let her know what was up. I gave Vonn a thousand and told him to give it to Nina Ross and tell her to go visit FN ASAP and let him know to sit tight and keep his mouth closed.

The fleeing and eluding were one thing, but there was absolutely no way they could prove his involvement in any other crime. So, he needed to sit tight and stay solid.

When I stepped inside Tori's house, she wasn't even home. I headed straight to my room and checked my stash. I had my two bags rigged in a way that would let me know if they had ever been tampered with in any type of way. That was an old habit. A quick inspection let me know all was well and nothing had been touched. Even though I have been here for nearly two months now. I still had yet to reveal my full fortune. And I probably never would.

It was obvious I had money and drugs, but much was undiscussed. So far, Tori was cool though and didn't seem to care about anything I had. Not even a little bit. She appreciated the gifts though and I could tell she loved being spoiled.

I stepped out of my clothes and took a long hot shower.

Once I felt clean and refreshed, I stepped out and dried off. I hung my towel on the rack and guided my naked body out of my personal bathroom. When I opened the door, Tori was sitting on my bed talking on her phone.

"Oh shit!" she quickly blurted and hung up her phone. Her eyes couldn't resist glancing down at the sight between my legs when she quickly rose from the bed. "I'm so sorry! I didn't expect you to come out naked," she bashfully stated.

Tori was wearing a baby blue jogging outfit, and the way the soft material hugged her hips and accentuated her curves looked delicious. Tori was beautiful and I couldn't help the natural reaction my body felt for her beauty.

Tori glanced down again and right before her eyes, my dick stretched out like Pinocchio just told a lie. She involuntarily gasped. She had never seen me with an erection, and I was a grower, not a shower.

The suddenly long length of my dick seemed to have Tori in a trance.

She eventually gathered her thoughts, looked me in the eyes and said, "Are you serious?"

"What?" I asked.

"What? Nigga, that big ass dick! That's what!"

I smiled and stepped closer to her. She didn't back away. Once I was directly in front of her, she reached out and grabbed my handle.

"Damn," Tori whispered.

I pulled her into my naked body and placed my lips over hers. For the first time, she didn't refuse my kiss nor push me away. Instead, she parted her lips and allowed my tongue to dance around in her mouth.

I guided her back to the bed and laid her down, carefully stripped her down to her birthday suit, and admired her naked body. I licked my lips, parted her thighs and had an instant urge to taste her. I dipped my head between her thick legs and slowly enjoyed the sweet taste of her juices.

"Oh, my fucking God," Tori moaned.

It didn't take much to get her dripping and I quickly brought her into a breathtaking orgasm. I licked my lips and pushed her trembling legs apart, spread her legs wide and slowly eased my dick inside of her body. She tried to lock her legs, but I held them firmly in place. Her mouth opened wide, and she moaned loudly as I slowly slipped deeper and deeper into her body. I was swimming in uncharted waters and her inner muscles squeezed my handle like a stress ball.

"Hold up! Shit! Wait..." Tori gasped.

Once I was balls deep, I slowly eased back and then re-entered her. After a few strokes long and deep, I repeatedly smashed myself into her body.

"Damn! Damn! Damn! Damn! Oh, my God, yes!" Tori shouted.

I continued to pound her until her eyes rolled into the back of her head and her thighs began to shake in my hands.

She was biting down on her bottom lip and feverishly rubbing her clit with one of her hands, while I continued to pound away.

Suddenly in mid-stroke, she shouted at the top of her lungs and her pussy exploded! A thick stream of liquid shot from her pussy and splashed against me. The sudden wetness and grip of her insides sent me over the edge, and I emptied a load of sperm inside of her. My body tensed up as I shot stream after stream into her goodies.

Once my dick stopped twitching, I pulled out and collapsed onto the bed. I glanced at Tori, and she had her eyes shut and her mouth open, while taking deep breaths.

"Yeah, it might be time for me to get the fuck up out of here," I joked.

Tori's eyes popped open, and she blurted, "What? Don't play with me! Yo ass ain't going a damn place now."

I smiled and blew her a kiss. She smiled back and sat up.

"Can we go out to eat please? I'm hungry," Tori asked me.

"Let me jump back in the shower real quick and then we can go to the moon, if that's what you want."

I headed back into the shower with one thing on my mind.

I finally fucked this bitch!

***

A week went by and nothing unordinary happened. Tori had a brand-new attitude ever since I baptized her with the dick. She was no longer shy or timid. Now, she was always tryna get up under me, and she didn't mind publicly displaying her affection.

Why do bitches always get clingy once you bless them with the dick?

Tori wasn't necessarily doing too much, but the change in her attitude was definitely evident.

Fat Nino was finally booked in the county jail yesterday. Me and Vonn had found out through his girl that FN had been hospitalized after the accident. He's alright, he just had a concussion. When we crashed, the airbag didn't deploy, and he smacked his head against the steering wheel.

When FN came to his senses, he was handcuffed to his hospital bed. The police had been there to question him multiple times and the youngin stayed solid.

When they questioned him about the murders, he played dumb and appeared to have no knowledge of what they were talking about. They asked him why he was driving on the same street where the murders took place and he denied ever being in the area, they told the officer on the scene upon his arrival.

FN said that couldn't have possibly been him because his car was dark blue, not black, and he had been riding alone. They asked him where he was coming from and where he was going, and his answer was coming from his girl's house. That was the only thing they could catch him in. When he arrived at the hospital, he had still been wearing the Magic City wristband.

Fortunately for him, it was a frivolous lie, because no one at the club had any recollection of three women or the boyfriend having ever been there. They had no way of connecting him to the murders in any way. They had tested his hands and clothes for gunpowder residue and both tests came back negative. He appeared to be innocent. Unless he had someone else in the car with him, but that was obviously something they would never know.

They eventually booked him anyway and processed him into the county jail yesterday. He was charged with a violation of probation, resisting without violence, and reckless driving.

That wasn't bad.

We couldn't bond him out because of the violation of probation, but I had Vonn give his girl enough money for a lawyer that would be able to get his probation reinstated, He was good.

Right now, I'm standing on the front porch at Tori's house, waiting for Vonn to scoop me up. He had called me about thirty minutes ago, and said he was coming through with the bread he owed me, and he wanted to re-up. In the process, I wanted to grab something to eat. I was starving and Tori was at work. It was definitely time for me to buy a car or at least keep a rental.

When Vonn pulled up, I jumped inside this black Mustang, and we pulled off.

"Look behind the seat," Vonn started while bending a corner.

I reached behind me and grabbed the only thing I felt. My efforts produced the same blue book bag Vonn had the day I met him. I unzipped the bag and eyeballed the many different bills that filled the bag. I re-zipped the bag and placed it between my feet on the floor of the car. I grabbed the brown shipping bag I brought with me and tossed it on Vonn's lap.

"That's two more birds," I stated. "I'll count this paper later when I get back to the house. You shouldn't need any more fronts after this."

"Bet that up, big homie," Von replied with a grin.

"Who is this car?" I questioned.

"This Con-Artist car."

"Con-Artist? Who the fuck is that? That nigga sound creepy as fuck."

"You ain't met bra yet. His real name Connie but we call him Con-Artist. The C-O-N stands for Cash Out Nino," Vonn explained.

I burst out laughing. "Bra, you niggas got some real clever ass names."

"You gotta be saucy when you're in the NBA!"

"NBA?"

"Nino Boy Association!"

I burst out laughing again. "How long it take y'all to come up with this shit? And, what y'all was smoking?"

Vonn joined my laughter.

"What's your clever name?" I asked.

"Hey, call me NV, but you pronounce it like 'Envy.' That means Nino Vee. Nobody calls me Vonn but you and my sister."

Vonn pulled into a Burger King drive-thru and while we were waiting in line, his phone rang.

"What's good?" Vonn answered.

Vonn was caught up in his phone conversation, so I had to tap him on the shoulder and signal him to drive up.

"Yeah, I got one for you right now actually," Vonn spoke while inching the car forward. "Yeah, I can do that…alright, I'm at the Burger King right down the street from you right now. Alright, I'ma park on the side, I'm in a black Mustang…Yeah, that's perfect…I call that…I got you...Grade-A, bra, you know that…Alright, bet."

Vonn ended his call and then pulled up to the window so I could place my order. After paying for my meal and receiving it at the next window, we parked on the side of the building, and I dug in.

"I got this dude about to meet up with us so I can serve him real quick," Vonn informed me.

"What is he coppin?"

"He want a whole block."

"A whole block? For how much?"

"He told me he got thirty for it right now. I told him I call that shit, that's a quick flip for me."

I nodded my head with approval and kept eating. Ten minutes later, a smoke-gray Chrysler pulled up beside us and a short, slim and geeky looking black kid with glasses hopped out and approached our car.

"That's him?" I questioned.

"Yeah, that's him," Vonn replied while rolling down his window.

The kid approached the open window and said, "What's good, my man? Everything-everything?"

"Yeah, I got you. Let me see that paper," Vonn replied.

"Alright, I got you. I just wanted to make sure we were handling business right here," the kid spoke and then turned back to his car.

"Bra, that lil geeky ass jit looks like he needs to be fixing somebody's computer, not buying no damn brick!" I stated.

Vonn laughed and said, "Yeah, he's young, he's still in high school. He go to a cracka school, but jit be out there waiting for them lil white kids."

"Man, fuck that. When *Dungeons and Dragons* come back to the car, tell him to hand you the money and then come on this side to grab the work from me."

The kid was already approaching Vonn's window, so Vonn had no time to reply or question my actions. The kid stuck a brown bag inside the car and dropped it on Vonn's lap. Vonn peeked inside and examined the tall stacks of hundreds.

"It's three stacks, each stack got ten grand in it," the kid stated.

"Alright, cool. Slide around the car and grab that work from my main man," Von spoke and nodded in my direction.

The kid bent down a little and peered inside the car to check me out. He saw the block sitting on my lap and started, "Uhm…alright, cool."

I rolled my window down and reached for my cannon. When the kid poked his head in my window, I quickly whipped my hand out and smacked him in the nose. His head snapped back, and his glasses fell off of his dorky-looking face.

"Ahh! What the fuck!" the kid shouted.

I stuck my arm out of the window with my Glock 17 in hand and blurted, "Get yo lame ass, pocket-protector wearing ass away from my car, jit!"

The kid picked his glasses up and when he saw my pistol, he nearly fainted.

"What the fuck, dude?" the kid shrieked.

"Jit, we ain't selling no dope to The Geek Squad! This shit took!" I barked. I looked at Vonn and blurted, "Why the fuck we still sitting here, nigga? Pull off!"

Vonn dropped the car and we smoothly drove away.

"Damn, big homie. You ain't have to smack the lil nigga. We could've just pulled off."

"I wanted to have fun with him first, but fuck that lil nigga, that was free money! We can use all the free money we can get. We gone bust that down, or I'll give you another block for half of the money. Take your pick."

"Hell, yeah! That's a sweet come up!"

Vonn's phone rang again and while he spoke, I thumbed through my newly obtained money. I had been doing a lot of spending lately and not enough gaining. I needed to change that.

"I'mma hit you back in like five minutes and let you know what's up," Vonn stated before ending his call. He then turned to me and said, "That was BNE, lil bra just scored on some fraud shit and hit me up, tryna grab some work."

"BNE? Breaking N Entering," I joked.

Vonn laughed and said, "That's what it's supposed to look like because he the youngest Nino, he turn eighteen in two weeks. But naw, his name stand for Baby Nino Eating."

"Alright, what he tryna do?"

"He said he just hit for fifty bands! He said it's a drag on the west side that wanna sell him twenty pounds of zaza for fifty, but he says he would rather buy some coke if I can plug him in. He wants to know IF I can get him two blocks for the fifty. I told him I'll hit him back in five minutes."

"Shit, hell yeah! Since he a Nino, I'll hook him up. Tell him you gone pull up on him right now, and to plug you in on the play for them twenty pounds. Just give him the two blocks I just gave you, and then when you drop me back off, I'll give you the two blocks back plus the other one for that fifteen. The dread with the twenty pounds we gone lay on and then take him up through there. Shit, that's free weed…How that sound?" I spoke.

"Sounds like a plan," Vonn replied while whipping his phone back out.

While Vonn politicked with BNE, I sat back and thought about my profits for the day. Over one hundred bands!

That's more like it!

Chapter 7

Another two months went by and now I was officially comfortable in my new environment. The last couple of months had been productive. Tori was coo-coo for Coco Puffs, and I found that funny. Considering how we met, I would've never expected her to be so fucked up about me.

Vonn and the Nino Boys had the streets looking like Christmas. They were letting snow fall everywhere and the money kept pouring in. Me and Vonn managed to rob the dread for them twenty pounds with ease. We also came out with an additional sixty grand that day,

Me and my lil soulja also managed to rob some white dude from town. We hit him for another fifteen pounds. With that, we've been able to put the weed game on lock as well. Things were going smoothly and all I had to do was sit back and collect, for the most part. I only got my hands dirty for a lick and when the time came for a lick, I only took Vonn, no extras.

Fat Nino had gotten out of jail a couple weeks ago. His probation had been reinstated, and I broke him off properly for keeping shit all the way solid and he was all smiles. He was definitely my Favorite Nino.

I was down to my last brick, but my bag was looking proper and continuing to grow with the work I had flooding the streets through the Nino Gang. Me and Vonn had two playsset up though, that might put my brick game back on top.

Vonn had met a nigga at the club and the nigga told Vonn he had heard about his squad and how they had been making it snow. They swapped info and the nigga told Vonn to hit him up when he was ready to cop then or better. You got to know I put that nigga on the top of my hit list.

Vonn had also heard about another nigga from out of town that was supposedly sitting on a mountain of cocaine.

A young nigga named Rone that Vonn used to go to school with was running with a clique of niggas from out of town in Riverdale, even though he lived in Atlanta. Rone had explained to Vonn that his crew had been shopping with the dude lately and although his business was good, he could be a target.

Rone knew how Vonn got down on the stick-up tip, so he told Vonn he would give him all the details he needed in order to hit the lick. He just wanted a fair cut. When Vonn presented the offer to me, I told him we would most definitely hit the clique, and depending on the outcome, we would then decide what would be a fair cut for Rone. So far, I ain't seen him getting any cut at all.

Other than that, I had met a new lil baby named Justice at a gas station one day and she had me wide open. Justice had a slim petite body, with a nice bubble butt that sat up and poked out. She had small firm breasts and smooth dark skin. Her body was beautiful and so was her face. Her nose, tongue and lip, and belly button were pierced. I later found out both her nipples and her pussy were also pierced.

Justice was about five-three and even though she had a small frame, she took the dick in every position like a pro. She was the perfect getaway whenever I got tired of Tori.

I had just left Justice's apartment and was now on my way to a Steak ‘n Shake to grab a little fuel for my belly. Being with Justice was a workout!

I was riding dolo. Yeah, I finally had wheels. I figured I’d just swap out rental cars every two weeks. I also had a phone finally and Tori was definitely annoyed.

Once I made it to the Steak ‘n Shake, I parked my whip and decided to go inside so I could relax while I ate. As soon as I entered, I was guided to a booth and seconds later, my waiter appeared and as soon as I saw her my jaw dropped.

“Dora?” I blurted.

Dora appeared to be just as surprised as I was, and she couldn't contain her smile. She was obviously happy to see me.

“Wizz! Oh my God! How are you? How have you been?” Dora rambled.

“Shit, I've been doing good and feeling good…no complaints on my end. I’m just focused on the money. How about you?”

"I've been maintaining it. I just got this job about a month ago. This is my second job and I do it part-time, so between this and my other job, I've been pretty much all work and no play."

I smiled. "Is that why you disappeared?"

"Disappeared? You the one disappeared…I was going to come back to Tori's house to see you about a week after we met, and Tori said you were gone."

"She said what?" I blurted.

"You sound surprised."

"What else did she tell you?"

"Nothing really…She just said you had left…She said when you were up and running you were in a rush to leave."

"When was the last time you saw her?" Now I was curious.

"I haven't seen her since I left that morning. So, I guess it's been a few months now. We talk on the phone, but she's been working a lot lately pulling doubles and doing overtime, so she's never home." In my head I was laughing. Tori was a slick motha-shut your mouth! I was wondering what I hadn't seen Dora again. Turns out Tori was cock blocking! Well, I wasn't going to fuck her game up.

"You gone sit down and keep me company while I eat?" I asked.

"I really wish I could, but I'm working. I'm off tomorrow though on both of my jobs, so we can hang out then if you want."

"Yeah, I'd like that," I stated while grabbing a menu.

I placed my order and allowed Dora to move around and tend to her other customers. Once she brought me my food, I ate quietly, and peacefully enjoyed my moment of solitude. When Dora returned to my table with the check, we swapped numbers and made plans for tomorrow. I then blessed her with a hundred-dollar tip and left.

When I got back to the house, Tori was chilling in the living room painting her nails. I flopped down beside her and rolled up a blunt.

"Hey bae," Tori spoke while keeping her attention on her nails.

"What's up, slickster?" I said with a grin.

Tori then looked up at me with a puzzled expression and said, “What's that supposed to mean?”

“I don't know the exact definition, but it’s basically a synonym for sneaky.”

“I know what the hell it means, smart ass…I mean, why is you calling me a slickster?”

I knew Dora would tell Tori she saw me, and I didn’t want to seem like the sneaky one in the end, so I decided to speak on it first, that way I seemed innocent in the long run.

“I went to get me something to eat earlier and guess who I bumped into?”

“Who?” Tori questioned.

“Dora.”

“Really?” Tori spoke in a shrill voice, with an expression that had “caught red-handed” written all over it.

“Yup, and she told me what you told her in regard to me *quote-unquote, urgently leaving.”* I smiled. “But don't worry, I played it cool, and I didn't blow your cover. I went along with your story and left it at that.”

Tori looked embarrassed and didn't speak,

“Cat got yo slick ass tongue?” I joked.

“Whatever! I wasn't being slick. My homegirl likes you and I don't want her messy ass to interfere with what we got going on.”

“That's under the table, but you told her I left before we even had anything going on,” I pointed out.

“Child, boo! You think I cleaned your ass every day and nursed you back to health, just so you could end up with my homegirl? Don’t make me hurt you,” Tori said with a serious face before laughing.

I leaned over and kissed her on the lips while smoke seeped from my mouth. “It's all good…You still qualify as a slickster though.”

After I smoked my blunt, I took a nap and got some rest before I linked up with Vonn tonight. Me, Vonn and a few of the Nino’s were supposed to be hitting the city tonight and having a little fun.

That meant nine times out of ten, I'd be wasted like a white boy tonight, so I needed to rest now.

***

I woke up around eight that night and had damn near twenty missed calls from Vonn, Justice and Dora. I took a quick shower and then got dressed in my usual multi-thousand-dollar attire. I decided to roll with a top to bottom Gucci outfit tonight, pants, shirt, shoes and bucket hat.

I stuffed five digits in my left pocket and then rolled up a blunt. I sat down in the living room and called Vonn.

"Damn, big bra! What's good? I've been blowing your shit up!" Vonn blurted as soon as he answered.

"I fucked around and passed out earlier. I was tired as fuck. I'm up and ready now though," I spoke.

"You're still steppin out with us, right?"

"Damn right! That's why I'm calling…who's all sliding?"

"It's gonna be me and you, FN and TNT, Nut and CNN, Con-Artist and my dawg Rone."

"Who the fuck is Nut and CNN?"

"Nut is the Nino that's from New York. Nut stand for Nino Up Top. CNN is Crazy Nigga Nino. Them the only two you ain't met yet. The only Ninos that ain't steppin out tonight is YFN- Young Fly Nino, SUN - Sauced Up Nino, and BNE. YFN and SUN got their own thing going on, and BNE ain't been answering his phone for the last couple days, I don't know what lil bra got going on."

"Alright, look so when we heading out?"

"We all gonna meet at CNN's house and then we swervin. You want me to come scoop you, or you want me to tell you how to get there?"

I thought about if for a moment then said, "Scoop me up, fuck it. I'll ride with you."

"Alright, I'm in traffic right now catching a quick play. Soon as I get done, I'ma head your way, I should be over there in about twenty or thirty minutes."

"Alright, say less." I ended the call and then hit Dora and Justice.

Dora wanted to make sure we were still on for tomorrow, and Justice wanted to know if she could get some dick tonight. One of them got a yes and one of them got a no.

When Vonn pulled up, I hopped in his whip, and we were off to the races.

"Damn, big bro! You always flexing on a nigga!" Vonn blurted while looking me over.

"What are you talkin 'bout?" I started while flashing my golden smile and holding up my glittering wrist.

Vonn was fly too, but he wasn't fucking with me. Without hearing his response, I cut the music up and began bouncing back and forth in my seat.

We arrived at CNN's house at 10:40 p.m. We hung out on the porch for a little bit and when the last attendant arrived, we all jumped back in traffic. CNN and Con-Artist rode in one car. FN, TNT and NUT rode in another. Me and Vonn stayed together and Rone rode dolo.

We headed downtown and hit the strip. TNT led the four-car line, and we followed him into the parking lot of a club that looked like it was way too packed to even get in. It was damn near midnight and the club line was crowded like they just opened the motherfucker. Not that it matters, it's already been established, I don't fuck with lines.

We approached the door and were quickly ushered inside after each of us paid a hefty price. I had to go back to the car because the bouncer was persistent about searching me. I tried to offer him a whole band just to let me slide through, but he wasn't budging.

We swarmed into the club and the perfect song was playing for my entry.

As soon as I heard the Future song screaming through the club, I immediately turnt up and started rapping along to the lyrics while bopping towards the dance floor. "Ayy! Gucci bucket hat! Gucci bucket hat! Ayy! Givenchy duffle bag! Givenchy duffle bag!" I had both of my hands on the brim of my Gucci bucket hat, while rocking back and forth through the crowds.

I looked around and saw my young companions bopping and getting lost all around me. The club lights had my diamonds dancing, and it didn't take long for a crowd of bitches to begin hovering around me and the gang. My youngins were making me proud.

A Lil Baby song began booming through the club and I couldn't help but show my ass for the bitches. I pulled out a fat stack of honchos, and fanned it at a group of women standing in front of me, while rapping the lyrics to the Lil Baby song.

"Come here, put that pussy on me…Don't be running from me…If I like it, I spend money on it…Get whatever from me."

An arm suddenly hung around my shoulder and when I looked over, it was my lil nigga FN. FN had a fat stack of hundreds in his hands and joined me in fanning the women with our wealth.

Right on cue the DJ, did us all a favor and let that throwback Juvenile pump through the speakers.

"Girl, you look good won't you back that ass up…You a fine muhfucka won't you back that ass up…Call me big daddy when you back that ass up…Girl who are you playing with back that ass up!"

Even though we weren't in any strip club, I couldn't help but to let a few bills fall on the thick chocolate honey that had her fat fluffy ass bouncing up against my lap. That Juvie gone do the trick every time.

I don't know if it was the knot in my pocket or my hard dick, but the chocolate honey felt something thick in my pants. I damn near lost my balance and stumbled back a little bit. I felt two sets of hands on my back and when I looked back, I saw FN and Vonn holding me steady. My youngins to the rescue.

I leaned all the way back and let my youngins hold me up while my chocolate freak did her thing and made that ass clap in my lap. Her ass was so fat, and it was shaking so much, her dress came up and when it did, the view from my vantage point was about to make me wife this hoe.

Another juicy looking redbone honey walked by and out of the corner of my eye, I saw CNN reach out and grab the baby on the ass, and I ain't talking about no slick sneaky grab. I'm talking about a big bold handful of ass. The redbone turned around and shouted something incomprehensible due to the loud music, but her body language was evident. She was not okay with that.

CNN'S drunk ass reached out for her again and her hand quickly whipped out and smacked him clean across his face. CNN then reflexively threw his hand back behind him and quickly shot it forward. Only difference between his hand and her hand was in a fist and the moment it made contact with her face, a loud pop noise echoed over the music and the woman suddenly flew into her home-girl and dropped to the ground.

Oh shit!

Everything else that happened after that happened so fast, I was unsure of some of it, but I know as soon as the redbone hit the floor, CNN got smacked across the head with a bottle and he hit the floor too. I then fell to the floor because Vonn and FN had suddenly dropped me, and my thick chocolate companion had fallen with me.

Somebody then flew over me and landed on the floor beside me and as I sprang to my feet, I noticed that whoever just flew over me like Superman was now being stomped and kicked by NUT and TNT. TNT then took a hard blow from his blind side, and he stumbled into me. As soon as I caught him, I was sucker punched from behind and pushed forwards. I stumbled into a crowd of niggas and fists started flying everywhere.

I took a couple hard blows to the face and a couple soft blows to the body during the fist frenzy, but I quickly gathered myself and started throwing haymakers. I wasn't aligned at any specific target, but I was clearly in the midst of the opps, and I needed to create some breathing room.

I made contact with somebody's mouth, and they dropped. Another dude dropped beside me, and I saw FN pounce on him. I saw a fist flying slowly towards my face and I effortlessly weaved it. I grabbed the dude and lifted him into the air. Somebody tackled me and the three of us crashed to the ground.

The lights came on in the club and the DJ screamed through the speakers, "Y'all cut this shit out!"

The music stopped and security was quickly on the scene, ripping us apart from each other. I threw a couple more punches and they connected with some black ass young nigga balled up underneath me. Security snatched me up and two of them put me in the chicken wing and dragged me to the door.

When they tossed me out, I quickly scrambled towards the car with one goal in mind, get my cannon! I looked back and saw Vonn scrambling behind me. When I went to the car, I grabbed my fye and started looking around. I don't know who the fuck them niggas was, but it just went down in that bitch and now I was ready to kill the parking lot. My adrenaline was pumping, and I was on go-mode with a full clip.

Vonn made it to the car and said, "Let's slide, bra! We don't need to get cased up out here! CNN and Con-Artist already took off and the rest of the boys are hopping in their wheels now."

We got inside the car and then followed TNT and them out of the parking lot. We all met up at CNN's house. Everybody except the nigga Rone.

"Them niggas got us fucked up!" CNN shouted while sitting in one of the chairs on the porch,

"Yo, fuck them niggas! I say we give then fuck niggas all the hell they looking for!" NUT barked in his up-top accent.

I looked around at the group and everybody was sporting some type of knot or bruise, busted lip, gash, or dirty shirt. Personally, I had a few knots on the back of my head and my left eye was feeling kind of clammy. I was straight though. My back had a sore spot, but I was mainly more pissed off about losing my Gucci bucket hat. Them niggas had to get it over that. It also seemed like I was the only person who wasn't aware of who the opps were. I don't like feeling left out.

"Who the fuck them niggas was?" I asked nobody in particular.

"Some fuck niggas from Riverdale," Vonn answered. "We don't really know them niggas like that, but that's them niggas Rone be fucking with."

"Y'all got beef with them niggas?" I had questions.

"We didn't, but we do now, thanks to this wild ass nigga CNN!" Con-Artist shouted.

"I ain't do shit!" CNN blurted. "That fuck nigga hit me cross the head with a damn bottle and you acting like it's my fault!"

"Nigga, your crazy ass knocked the nigga bitch slap out!" Con-Artist blurted back.

"Fuck him and his bitch! And fuck all them niggas! That shit on and poppin now!" CNN barked with his anger on full display. CNN patted the gash on top of his head and stared at the blood in his hands. He then stormed inside of his house and left the door swinging

I rolled up a fat ass Backwood and put the blunt in rotation. TNT and FN also rolled up, so we had three blunts going around. CNN eventually came back out with a rag on his head and joined the smoke session. We all smoked and calmed our nerves and after another session with three more blunts, we were all high as fuck, tired as fuck, and ready to head home.

I hopped in the whip with Vonn and the two of us headed to McDonald's. After knocking down a triple quarter pounder and a king-sized box of fries, I was ready to tap out.

Thirty minutes later, Vonn dropped me off in front of Tori's house and swerved off. I entered the house, lazily wobbled my way to Tori's room and stripped down naked. I didn't want to climb into the bed with Tori while I had all this filth on me, so I took a quick five-minute shower and then climbed into the bed butt ass naked.

Once Tori felt my presence in the bed, she reached out and grabbed my body. She pulled herself close to me and snuggled up against my naked flesh. She put her head on my chest and went right back to snoring. Seconds later, I too, was out like a light.

Chapter 8

I woke up bright and early to the pleasure of Tori stuffing my dick in her mouth. She didn't have the capability of deep throating though. She would always gag if my dick went too deep into her mouth. She got drunk one night and tried to just go for it and ended up throwing up all over the floor. She was embarrassed, but I thought it was funny. I let her know she didn't have to feel embarrassed, and I thought her effort was a turn-on.

Even though Tori couldn't deep throat, it was all good because of the way she passionately made love to the amount she could manage. It was always a beautiful sight and a wonderful feeling.

Tori sucked me dry and when I came in her mouth, she casually got up and pranced into the bathroom to spit the nut out. She never swallowed the nut, that wasn't her thing. She didn't mind catching it, but she thought actually swallowing it was nasty. She said she didn't like the taste and the way it felt going down made her sick. As long as I busted my nut, I couldn't care less what she did with it. By the time she brushed her teeth and crawled back into the bed with me I was already back in the dream world.

I woke up again about two hours later and jumped into the shower. Tori joined me and let me know she was heading to work early because she had some type of training she had to do. Fine by me. When we got out of the shower she got dressed and off she went.

I called Dora to let her know I was up and running and she gave me the directions to her house. Within an hour, I was on the doorstep and calling her to let her know I was outside. When she opened the door, I was instantly reminded of her beauty that captivated me the day I woke up and met her.

I gave her a hug and kissed her on the cheek. She led me inside and told me to make myself comfortable while she finished getting ready. We were scheduled for a reservation at some sort of fancy restaurant downtown. I had never heard of the place, but Dora said she had always wanted to go there and try their food so fuck it, I made a reservation.

Dora was already dressed in a knee-length summer dress and looking good, so I wasn't exactly sure what she meant by *finish getting ready,* but whatever it was it had taken her twenty minutes to accomplish. When she finished, we stepped out and hopped in my rental. I didn't know where the place was, so I played the passenger seat and let Dora drive.

We arrived about ten minutes early. Once we were seated and eating, our vibe came naturally, and I was actually enjoying Dora's company. We kept each other laughing and we got to know each other on a more personal level. She told me about her background and her past, and I shed a little light of mine. Very little. She noticed my reluctance when it came to discussing things about myself during certain topics, but she wasn't certain she was cool about it. The way we met let her know I was rough around the edges and had an untold story, but she didn't seem to care. Nor did she question me about my relationship with Tori.

We ate and afterwards, we went to a mall and I decided to blow a couple bands on her. I had a bad habit of flexing and blowing money on women I like...

It ain't trickin if you got it though right!

Dora definitely didn't expect to be pampered or lavishly treated when we went to the mall. She thought we were just going to walk around and vibe, but to her surprise, I bought her every single thing she liked and by the end of our shoppin spree, she was at a loss for words.

Once we were back on the road, I was leaning back in my seat and contemplating what we should do next. I wanted to either catch a movie or go bowling. I don't usually get a chance to do these types of minor things and I was feeling the energy between me and Dora, so I wanted to keep hanging out for a while.

Her phone suddenly went off and at first, she ignored it but when it immediately rang a second time, she decided to answer for the number she claimed to not recognize. The caller turned out to be her auntie and the number turned out to be from the county jail.

Dora's auntie had served a simple thirty days in the county jail for repeatedly driving without a license. She was now free and in need of a ride. Dora tried saying she was busy, but the lady on the other end of the phone insisted she had no other ride and she needed her. I let Dora know it was okay and we could go get her and take her wherever she needed to go, so Dora told her aunt to sit tight, and she would be there.

We were way on the other side of town by this time, but it was all good, I was just chilling. I rolled a blunt and smoked while Dora made a U-turn and maneuvered through traffic. We eventually arrived at the county jail and Dora stepped out of the car to flag down her auntie and signal her over.

During that quick moment, I noticed a very familiar red Lexus parked a few cars ahead of us and instinctively eased deeper into my seat to remain unnoticed.

What the fuck is she doing here?

Another surprise suddenly hit me, and I witnessed the lil nigga BNE come strolling out of the county doors and head straight for the familiar red Lexus.

BNE had a small bag of property in his hand and a folder full of paperwork. He hopped in the passenger seat of the Lexus, and I leaned back as they drove by and pulled off.

What the fuck?

So that's why jit ain't been answering his phone since he's been sitting in the county jail.

I wonder why he ain't call nobody and let them boys know he was fucked up?

Whatever it was it must have been minor because he was out now, so I guess jit was straight. I wanted to hop out real quick and show some love to the lil Nino, but I didn't want the bitch he jumped in the car with to see me.

Dora's auntie then climbed into my back seat, and she smelled just like the county jail. The cheap ass deodorant she was wearing was useless.

Dora introduced us and then we pulled out of the parking lot. I offered to buy her some food and she happily accepted the offer. She wanted some Popeyes chicken, so we took her to Popeyes and then took her home.

Now we were back at Dora's house, and she was putting away all of her new clothes and accessories. When she finished doing that, she poured us some wine and we kicked back in the living room.

"I had so much fun today and I really enjoyed your company. I work so much it seems like I never have enough time for genuine enjoyment," Dora stated while sipping her glass of wine.

"I can toast to that," I said while raising my glass.

Dora tapped her glass against mine and we both took another sip. She then swung her legs over me and straddled my lap. I lifted her dress up and put my arms around her. She leaned into me for a kiss, and I grabbed hold of her round bubbly ass cheeks.

Her kiss was electric and filled with passion. Right when the mood was beginning to heat up, my phone started vibrating in my pocket. I ignored the vibration and continued my French kiss. As soon as my phone stopped vibrating, it started again, and Dora stared at me to see what I gonna do.

Somebody picked a fucked-up time to be with the bullshit!

I wiggled my phone out of my pocket and noticed Vonn was calling. The phone had stopped ringing by the time I fished it out of my pants, so I decided to send him a quick text to let him know I was busy. Before I could send the text, he was calling again so I quickly answered.

"Damn, lil nigga, what's up? You fucking up my vibe!" I blurted.

"What's good, big bra? Listen, I got Rone with me right now and bra say it's the perfect time to hit the lick on that nigga he was telling us bout! He say his dawg them just dropped off a boatload of money and when they got there, the nigga was drunk as fuck and chilling with some hoe. He off beat like a motherfucka and it's the perfect time to hit," Vonn explained.

"What the fuck you doing with Rone? Ain't he rocking with the opps?" I questioned.

"Bra straight. Yeah, he fuck with them clowns but I already told you how me and bra go back. He don't want no parts of that, he good."

"I don't know about all that...Jit might be tryna set yo ass up."

"He good, bra, I'm telling you. He already explained to me his side of things. But what's up, bra? What are we gone do? We gone hit or what?"

"This shit can't wait until tomorrow?" I asked while rubbing on Dora's thigh with my free hand.

"I told you, big bra, the perfect time to strike is now! Bra done gave me all the details already. I got the whole layout and the run-down. As soon as we link up. I'll give you the play book."

"Fuck!" I blurted. "Alright, where you wanna meet at?"

"Just slide over here since you already out. In at my spot."

"When you tryna make this shit happen?"

"Right now, big bra! The sun already going down, by the time we get everything ready and roll out, the timing should be perfect."

"Alright jit, damn…I ain't too far from you right now, so give me like thirty minutes and I'll be there." I hung up the phone and didn't bother hearing a response.

I was definitely annoyed, but the saying is, Money Over Bitches! Me personally, I like to say *Pop Over Pussy!* Same shit.

Dora looked extremely annoyed and had a childish pout on her face.

"My bad, but when the money call, I gotta go," I stated.

Dora climbed off of my lap and said, "It's okay, I guess...I understand. It was still a great day." I could hear the disappointment in her voice.

"I got one more thing for you before I go," I spoke.

I rose from the couch and fixed my pants. I then leaned her back on the couch and gave her a kiss on the lips, grabbed both of her legs and lifted them in the air. Her dress fell up and revealed her smooth thighs and white lace panties.

I kissed her right ankle and planted a trail of kisses down her leg until I reached her puffy pussy, when my lips brushed against the lacy fabric, she moaned lightly. I pulled her panties off and kneeled on the floor between her legs. I then pushed her legs back and instructed her to hold her legs back like she was about to give birth.

She did as she was told, and her gorgeous pussy was propped up right in my face and looked delicious. Dora was biting her bottom lip with anticipation and since I was technically in a rush, I didn't hesitate to dive in. I had to make this quick.

I started off by licking her entire pussy and making sure she was soaking wet, then I wrapped my lips around her large clitoris, poking out and demanding attention. I began licking and sucking on it like a nipple. Dora's moans because louder and her head was tilted back. She was riding the waves of ecstasy and loving every moment of it.

I slipped two fingers inside of her and pumped them in and out while continuing to lick and suck her throbbing clit.

"Ooooh shit! Damn, daddy! Yes! Stay right there! Stay right there! Shit! Fuck! I'm bout to cum, daddy! I'm bout to cum! Here it come, baby! Here it comes! Fuck!" Dora screamed.

Her thighs began to vibrate, and her pussy got wetter and wetter. I squeezed her clit with my lips and that was all it took. Her inner juices flooded my face and created a puddle on the couch beneath her. She let out one final moan and it was so loud, I'm sure her neighbors heard it.

"Damn!" Dora panted like she was out of breath.

I gave her pussy one last kiss and then rose back to my feet. She still had her legs cocked back and I was tempted to drop my pants and drop that dick in her, but I had to go.

Dora let her legs fall and her feet slammed down on the floor. "That was the best head I ever had in my life!" Dora sighed. "Hands down."

"I was really just getting started," I boasted with a smile. "I gotta slide though. I just wanted to make sure you were at least slightly satisfied for the moment."

"Hell yeah, nigga! I'm about to take my ass to sleep and dream about that shit again."

"Alright," I laughed. "I'll catch up with you whenever you're free again. Just hit me up, I gotta go." I gave her a quick peck on the lips and headed for the door.

Before I walked out, Dora grabbed my face and give me another one of those extremely passionate kisses.

This bitch gone fuck around and make me abort mission.

I pushed her back gently and said, "Alright, damn…let me go!"

Dora laughed and waved me off. She stood in the doorway until I was gone. As I headed to Vonn's apartment, I knew I had Dora hooked. She'd be calling me soon.

Chapter 9

I pulled up to Vonn's apartment and hopped out of my whip. I stretched out and cracked my back. My body was kind of sore from the brawl last night and that let me know I'd been neglecting my physical fitness. I needed to get back on my regular work-out routine.

When Vonn opened the door, I stepped inside of his small apartment and noticed the nigga Rone sitting on the couch. I gave him a disapproving look and sat on the other couch. Nina Alina came out of one of the rooms for a split second to get something out of the kitchen. She waved at me and then returned to the room.

I peeped Vonn's all-black attire and realized I wasn't even properly dressed for the occasion.

"What's good, big bro?" Vonn blurted with excitement. "You ready to go get this money?"

"Nigga, ain't I here? What kind of dumb ass question is that? Nigga, do dogs bark?" I questioned him back.

Vonn laughed and said, "You look like you're on yo way to a dinner date or some shit."

"I told you I was busy! You cockblocked a nigga!"

"Well, you can make love to this money tonight. This gone be a real come up," Vonn eagerly spoke.

"What do we pose to be hitting for?" I quizzed.

"We don't know exactly what the nigga sittin on, but the nigga sitting pretty…Real pretty," Vonn explained.

"Nigga, what! We bout to hit a blind lick? You got me running in a nigga shit and you done even know what's in it? Nigga, I ain't seventeen! A nigga don't do no dumbass shit like that no more! That's how you get killed!"

"Rone say his scrub ass homeboys done bought seven bricks from this nigga, and them seven bricks seemed like peanuts to the nigga. I'd call that probable cause to trip check," Vonn stated.

"Let me hear this playbook," I stated while shaking my head.

"Give big bra the layout," Vonn said to Rone.

Rone finally spoke for the first time since I've been here. "The nigga stay in a two-bedroom house. It ain't no fancy place and it ain't no fancy neighborhood. It's pretty average so y'all ain't gotta worry about no nosy neighbors or no shit like that. Sometimes the nigga be having other niggas around, but most of the time he rolls by himself. He normally acts real edgy and paranoid, but tonight he's off his rocker and loose.

"The nigga stay strapped so you can't play with him, unless he just packing for show, but you still gotta be aware of that. The nigga ain't tall, average height, but he cocky as fuck so I doubt he a weak nigga. I'm pretty sure he keeps his stash in one of the two rooms, I don't know which one though.

While I was over there earlier with my dawgs and they were coppin, I had slipped off into the bathroom and unlocked the window. The window is on the left side of the house and y'all can fit through it.

"That's why it's a plus that he's drunker than a bitch. It might sound like some hot boy shit, but once y'all creep into the spot and get the ups on him y'all straight…Y'all gone need a third man though to make it smoother and faster. While one of y'all hold the nigga down, the other two can split up and check both of the rooms...Shit, that's pretty much it."

Vonn looked at me and said, "So what's up, big homie…What you think?"

I paused for a moment then said, "You've gotta be kidding me."

"You ain't feeling that?" Vonn questioned.

"Ain't no fucking way a nigga with a mountain of cocaine gone be that damn sweet! Where the fuck they do that at?" I shook my head and looked at these two niggas like they were crazy.

"And who the fuck gone be the third man?" I questioned.

"I told Rone he should slide with us since he already knows the layout, but he say he don't wanna be on the scene since the nigga know him," Vonn spoke.

"So, fucking what! You think we gone rob a nigga for a mountain of cocaine and just let the nigga go on bout his business? Fuck no! You might as well go in!" I blurted at Rone.

"I can't lie, big bro, robbing and shit ain't really my field. I don't wanna get in the way and fuck y'all up. That's the real reason I don't wanna do it," Rone admitted.

I shook my head and looked at Vonn. I guess I had to respect the nigga honesty. If he didn't have the balls to hit the sack, then he simply did not have the balls. I definitely wasn't tryna slide with no scary ass rookie with marble balls.

"This shit sounding flakier and flakier by the minute," I stated.

"So, what do you wanna do?" Vonn questioned. "It's yo call, big bra. I ain't doing shit if you say it's a no-go."

"Man, go grab me some sack chasing clothes, lil bra. I ain't slide over here and cancel my damn date for nothing! And call Lil FN…That's gone be our third leg," I spoke.

Vonn hustled into his room and quickly came back out with some black sweatpants and a black thermal top. After I slipped into the black wardrobe, Vonn tossed me a black skully and some black gloves.

"I called FN and told bra to be on point. We gone swing by his spot and scoop him up. Once we grab bra we gone head straight out," Vonn spoke.

"And what bout this nigga?" I asked and pointed at Rone.

"Bra going home. We gone link back up with him tomorrow so he can get his cut," Vonn explained

I shrugged my shoulders and looked at my watch. It was getting late. "Let's do it," I concluded.

***

Me, Vonn, and FN were silently riding in the car, on our way to the address provided by Rone. It took us hours to reach our destination, but once we made it, we were all hyped and ready to make it happen. I created a slightly new plan along the way, and I made sure the three of us had it down pat.

We parked in the driveway of a vacant house down the street and as we approached our target's house on foot, I found it hard to believe a nigga with a ton of bricks lived inside it. We immediately rushed to the side of the house and squatted down behind an AC unit. We quickly jumped the back gate and then landed a few feet away from the bathroom window. It took FN's fat ass a little more effort and time to hit the gate then me and Vonn, but he made it.

Since me and Vonn had the same slim build, we were going to go through the window and try to peep the inner layout. Once me and Vonn were inside, it would be FN's job to create a slight disturbance on the other side of the house. After that, the plan would be in motion and there would be no turning back.

I checked the window and as promised, it was unlocked. I slowly and quietly eased it up and peeked inside. I couldn't see shit except for a bathtub and enclosed shower curtain. I told Vonn to give me a boost and then I slowly eased my way through the slim, rectangular-shaped window.

Once I got my upper body inside, I looked around and didn't see a way for me to ease myself down into the tub. The window wasn't wide enough for me to turn around and swing my legs over, so I slowly eased back out and then told Von to boost me in backwards. This time I eased myself through the window legs first and eased in, until my foot made contact with the soap holder molded into the wall.

I balanced one foot on that and then eased my other foot down onto the ledge of the tub. Once my feet were planted, I was able to let my weight fall in and ease into the bathtub.

Alright, that worked out.

FN then boosted Vonn through the window the same way and I helped ease him down once he was on my side. We stepped out of the tub and gave FN the signal to head around to the other side of the house.

The bathroom we were in was at the end of the hallway with two bedrooms on each side. The long hallway led to the living room and a kitchen, beyond that was a garage.

The only entrances to the house were through the front door, the garage, and the glass sliding back door. FN was headed for the sliding glass door.

Me and Vonn stood in the dark bathroom with our cannons in hand and quietly waited to hear the signal that would get the party started. I listened intently and didn't hear anything, except a TV playing in the distance somewhere in the house. Like a minute later, Me and Vonn heard a low whistle coming from the window we just climbed through.

I signaled to Vonn to stay quiet while I tip-toed back in the tub and peeked out the window. FN was standing there with his pistol out. I gave him a "*what the fuck*" expression.

"I saw the nigga through the glass door," FN whispered.

"He is lying in the living room on the couch with a chick. It looks like they are just watching TV. It's dark in there and the TV is the only light."

Shit, alright...That makes shit easier. No diversion needed. We already know where the nigga at.

"Alright, just post up by the door and when you see Vonn do his thing, bust in and run back here to the rooms and be quick. Take the room on the right, I'm in the room on the left," I instructed FN.

FN slipped off while I quietly returned by Vonn's side.

"FN say the nigga laying down on the couch in the living room with a bitch. This what we gonna do...You should be able to get the ups on the nigga by yourself. Just run off in that bitch and put the pistol on him. Pop that nigga in the leg or something if you got to. I'ma go straight for the room and check the trap. FN gone bust in and join me. After we find the treasure, go ahead and smoke that nigga boots...him and the bitch...Ready?" I whispered.

"Let's get paid," Vonn whispered back.

I slowly twisted the bathroom doorknob and eased it open. I peeked out into the dark hall and made a quick scan.

The bedroom door on the left was already open and the right was closed. The TV in the living room was more audible now and it sounded like either they were watching a flick or doing more than watching TV. Vonn would definitely have the upper hand if he caught the nigga with his pants down.

I dashed into the left bedroom and signaled for Vonn to make his move. Vonn quietly scurried ahead of me and made his way down the hall. I listened intently to make sure he successfully accomplished his part of the plan.

Vonn eased up to the corner of the hallway and peeked around the corner, the man and woman were cuddled up on the couch. The nigga had his shirt off and appeared to be sleeping. The woman had her arms wrapped around the nigga and was wide awake watching a movie. The movie was playing a sex scene.

Vonn quickly zoomed into the open space and aimed his gun directly at the woman. The woman screamed and tried to jump up but was weighed down by the man's body. The man suddenly jumped up and his red eyes were as wide as golf balls.

"Nobody moves, nobody gets hurt," Vonn coolly spoke like he was in a movie or some shit.

Suddenly the sound of glass shattering echoed through the house and FN flew into the living room.

"You good?" FN asked Vonn.

"Yeah, I got it," Vonn answered.

I then began quickly flipping through the usual spots and hiding places. While throwing shit around, I looked up and saw FN quickly creep into the room I was in.

"What the fuck you doing, jit?" I barked.

"You told me to hit the room on the right," FN replied.

"Nigga, your fat ass don't know your right from your left?"

"This is the room on the right side of the hallway!"

I thought about it and realized that since he came from the opposite direction, I should've told him to go left.

"Well, go to your other right!" I blurted.

FN dashed out the room and ran into the hallway. He quickly pushed into the room across the hall and instantly a loud bang echoed through the air. When I looked up, I saw FN flip back into the hallway and land flat on his back.

Oh, shit!

I quickly ran to the side of the door and crouched down.

Boom! Boom!

Two loud shots suddenly rang out in the living room.

Bang! Bang! Bang!

Three more shots went off from a different caliber pistol.

What the fuck was going on?

I peeked around the door and saw FN lying lifelessly in a pool of blood.

Damn!

Suddenly I saw movement through the opposite door, so I aimed through the darkness and when the shadow moved again, I pulled the trigger twice.

Boom! Boom! Boom! Boom!

A groan and a thud quickly followed behind my shots, and I knew my bullets found their mark.

Tat-Tat-Tat-Tat-Tat-Tat-Tat-Tat-Tat-Tat!

Oh, shit! Shit was going down in the living room!

I peeked down the hallway and saw Vonn shoot through the gap and dive towards the glass door. I quickly shuffled back into the room and hurried towards the window.

I bust the lock on the window, threw the window up and dove out. I landed in some bushes, but quickly sprang to my feet and hauled ass down the street. I heard something behind me and when I looked back, I saw Vonn hightailing it like a track star.

We reached the car seconds apart and once we were both in, we put the pedal to the metal and zoomed off. I had the key, so I was driving. Vonn was lucky. I fuck with jit the long way, but if he wasn't behind me when I made it to the car, his ass would've been left. Too many gunshots had gone off and I had no way of knowing his fate. Plus, the only fate that really needed to be secured at all times was mine!

"What the fuck happened?" Vonn blurted once we were safely on the road and headed back towards his apartment.

"Mission failed!" I blurted.

"What the fuck though? I had the nigga held down, then next thing I know I heard a shot ring out in the hallway."

"Yo flaw ass homeboy Rone gave us some fucked-up information!" I shouted. "It turned out to be somebody in the other back room and as soon as FN went in, he got popped."

Like I said before, FN was my favorite Nino. That nigga Rone just made my hit list! Whether it was done intentionally or by default, it didn't matter…I had to have him!

"Damn!" Vonn shouted and slammed his fist down on the dashboard.

We made the rest of the trip in silence. I was lost in my thoughts and Vonn was lost in his. Even though I had grown a little fond of FN, I could only imagine what Vonn was feeling. I had just lost a little soulja, but Vonn had just lost a brother.

Once we were back at Vonn's spot, I stepped inside for a moment but didn't want to slip back to Tori's house tonight, so I whipped out my phone and called Justice.

"What's up, bae?" Justice answered.

"You home?"

"Mm-hmm…Why?"

"I'll be there in a little bit," I stated then hung up the phone.

Chapter 10

Justice opened the door wearing a big white T-shirt that went down to her thighs. She stepped to the side to let me in and as I brushed past her, she rolled her eyes.

"You curved me last night, avoided me all day, and now you wanna pop up on me at three o'clock in the morning?" Justice said in a groggy voice.

"Better late than never…Quit complaining," I stated while removing my shirt and crashing down on the couch.

"Nigga, whatever. I'm going back to sleep." Justice rolled her eyes again and walked back to her room.

It had been a long day and an even longer night. The last thing I wanted to hear right now was a bitch complaining. That's why I decided to come here instead of Tori's house.

I stretched out on the couch and stared at the roof. Flashbacks of my uneventful night flowed through my mind like a river, and I couldn't help but think about the unfortunate fate of Fat Nino.

Dammmmn.

My mind continued to show me a series of unwanted images until I slipped into a much-needed sleep.

***

When I woke up, Justice was sitting on the couch across from me, smoking a blunt. I laid still for a moment before finally sitting up.

"What bitch got you tired like that?" Justice blurted.

"I ain't tryna hear that fuck shit," I spoke while stretching.

I then stood up, glided over to where she was sitting and snatched the blunt from her hand without asking. I took a deep pull and handed it back to her.

"Fix a nigga something to eat. I'm finna take a quick shower," I stated and headed for her bedroom.

On my way to the bathroom, I peeped the time displayed on the clock on her dresser. It was almost one o'clock in the afternoon.

I knew I was tired, but damn!

After a quick ten-minute shower, I put on some clothes that I kept at her spot and slipped back into the living room. Justice was in the kitchen getting busy over the stove for me, looking fine as ever in her Adidas tracksuit.

I pulled up behind her and threw my arms around her slim waist. I pressed my dick up against her soft bubble butt and gave her a gentle kiss on the side of her neck.

"You got it smelling good for a nigga," I spoke.

"After the way you just slept, I figured you could use a nice full course meal."

"Do ya thang, bae." I smacked her on the ass. "Oh yeah, and ain't no bitch got me tired. I had a long night with my lil nigga. We got tied up in some bullshit and everything went sour."

"It's all good. I was just playing…Okay, I was just playing, but I smelled yo dick while you was sleeping so I know you wasn't fucking around."

I shook my head and Justice smiled. I stepped over to the table in the kitchen and gave her some room to work her wrist. I took a seat and began rolling a blunt. While rolling up, I noticed a stack of papers on the table to my right and then I instantly remembered I had seen this bitch at the county jail yesterday, picking up BNE!

This bitch got the nerve to question my whereabouts? Justice was twenty-six. What the fuck was she doing with that young ass nigga? Was jit fucking my bitch?

I grabbed the stack of papers and began slowly reading and flipping through them. Justice saw me reading the paperwork but didn't seem to care.

"Who do these papers belong to?" I questioned.

"My lil brother," Justice answered without looking up.

Her lil brother? What the fuck?

"If they belong to yo lil brother, then what the fuck they doing way over here?" I probed.

"I had to pick him up yesterday from the county jail and when I dropped him off at our mother's house, he had left the papers in my car. I brought them in the house with me and put them there. I forgot to tell him about it. Couldn't be too important if he left them in my shit in the first place."

"What's his name?" I asked, even though I just read his name on the papers.

"Toydel. You wouldn't know him. He just turned eighteen."

"He in the streets?"

"If that's what you wanna call it. That was his first time being locked up."

"What do they call him?"

"Some weird ass shit. Baby Nino something. I don't know. We got the same mom, but different dads. He grew up with his dad, so I don't really know him as well as my other siblings."

Small fucking world.

I started to tell her I knew her lil brother, but something strange caught my attention. I already saw he had been charged with possession of cocaine, which was no surprise since I had just sold the lil nigga two bricks. But now I was reading his police report and to my surprise, jit had gotten caught with a whole block! Who the fuck gets caught with thirty-six ounces of cocaine and walks out of jail a couple weeks later? Shit, he is supposed to be on his way to the feds right now.

I kept scrolling through the large stack of papers and saw a report from an agent. The words *Drug Enforcement Agency* were printed across the top of the report. I began reading and began shaking my head.

Tsk-Tsk-Tsk-Tsk-Tsk-Tsk-Tsk-Tsk.

This fuck nigga Baby Nino Eating was a confidential informant! He struck a deal with the DEA to take down his supplier in exchange for immunity and future cooperation.

Bitch ass muthafucka!

The DEA had gotten an order from the judge to release him into their supervised custody.

As far as BNE knew, his supplier was Vonn, but unknowingly, the supplier was me!

This couldn't be good.

I kept flipping and came across a group of printed pictures. The pictures were clearly surveillance photos because they were all taken from odd angles, and none of the occupants in the photos seemed to notice that they were being photographed. I slowly flipped through the photos and shook my head. *The NBA was in full attendance. CNN, TNT, NUT, YFN, Con-Artist, SUN, FN, and above all, Vonn!*

How did he get a copy of these photos, I wondered.

Even though there were pictures of everybody, it was evident Vonn was the main focus of the investigation. They had him at his apartment, the mall, a subway and a red light, a McDonald's and at TNT's house, and then I nearly fell out of my seat! They had a picture of Vonn coming out of Tori's house and guess who else was in the picture…me!

The picture was clearly about Vonn, but sure enough, I was in the background walking behind him. Even though I was in the background, it was broad daylight, and I was clearly visible. There was one more photo of me and Vonn getting inside a car, but I wasn't as noticeable in that one. I was already crouching in the car and Vonn had just begun opening his door.

Justice noticed the sudden change in my expression and began walking toward the table. I quickly put the papers back together and pushed them to the side where I had found them.

"You alright?" Justice asked. "You look upset. You seemed like you were in a fairly good mood a few minutes ago. Now you got ya face all scrunched up like a Sour Patch Kid."

"Yeah, I'm cool, baby. I was just zoned out, thinking about the bullshit from last night I was telling you about," I lied.

"Well, whatever happened, don't let it stress you, bae. Yo food gone be done in about five minutes."

Justice got up and went back to the stove and I leaned back in the wooden chair I was sitting in. I fired up the blunt I had rolled and took a long drag. The smoke instantly invaded my mind and thoughts. This was a bad situation and it needed to be nipped in the bud immediately.

Fuck!

***

After I ate my home cooked meal and blew Justice's back out, Vonn had called me stating the nigga Rone had just hit him up, asking about the lick. He wanted his cut. Obviously, shit hadn't hit the fan yet and he was unaware of what had happened, so Vonn told him to hold up while he hit me up. I told Vonn to tell Rone we would link up with him later on in the night, because I didn't want to be riding around with all that work in broad daylight. Rone happily agreed and said he would be waiting on our call.

I then told Vonn I had some serious shit I needed to holla at him about and it couldn't wait, so we needed to link up ASAP! He told me he was at a Con-Artist's house, so I told him to sit tight, and I'd be over there shortly.

Justice had tapped out and went to sleep after I hit her with that magic stick, so I quietly slipped out of the house and left her right where she was at. I was now on the road and resting in my passenger seat, was a few of the papers I had taken out of BNE's paperwork. I didn't need all of it and I didn't want Justice to know I had it, so I simply took the pages I needed to show proof of my accusations when I pulled up on Vonn.

Halfway to Con-Artist's house my phone rang, and it was Vonn.

"Yo!" I answered.

"Bra, slide to the hospital!" Vonn shouted. "Con-Artist just got shot!"

Before I could respond to Vonn's frantic comment, the line went dead.

What the fuck?

I quickly made a U-turn and headed towards the hospital. When I got there, I called Vonn and told him to come outside and meet me in the parking garage. I didn't want to be seen with him and all of his homies that I'm sure were piling into the hospital.

When Vonn approached the garage, I honked my horn to let him know where I was and when he got to my car and slid into my passenger seat, I instantly noticed he was covered in blood.

"Damn, lil bra! What the fuck?" I spoke. "I thought y'all was at bra's house waiting on me?"

"We was sitting on the porch and them fuck niggas from the club spinned the bend and shot that shit up," Vonn wearily explained. "I dove to the ground and tried to bust back, but them niggas had gotten hit and was bleeding bad. I tossed him in his car and rushed him here."

"Damn," I mumbled, "who all here?"

"Just TNT and CNN, but they are about to leave soon. Right now, they're just showing their condolences to Con-Artist's mama and sister. Right before you got here, the doctor came out and told us I didn't get bra to the hospital fast enough. He didn't make it."

A tear fell down Vonn's face and he quickly wiped it with the back of his hand.

I shook my head and drove off.

"This ain't the best time but it can't wait though. Check the papers out you put on the floor when you got in," I spoke to Vonn while driving us back to his place.

Vonn slowly scooped up the papers and began reading them. After he read a few pages and realized what he was seeing, he stopped reading and looked at me.

"Ain't no fucking way," Vonn mumbled.

"It's in black and white, lil bra, believe it. That's why I ain't tell you, instead I let you read it for yourself…Keep flipping through it," I instructed.

Vonn continued to flip through the pages and when he got to the pictures, he examined each one closely. One picture had both FN and Con-Artist in it together and as Vonn stared at the photo, another tear slid down his face. This time, he didn't wipe it.

Once we made it to Vonn's apartment, I reached into the backseat and grabbed a hoodie. I slipped it on and then entered the apartment with Vonn. Vonn quickly made his way into his room and disappeared behind the door. Moments later, I heard the shower running.

I rolled up a fat blunt of that gas and waited for Vonn to finish getting himself together. When he returned to the living room and joined me on the couch, I fired up the blunt and tossed it to him. I could tell he really needed it.

"So, what's good, big bra? What the fuck we gone do? It's so much shit going on right now, I can't even think straight! I need some guidance, big homie. Talk to me," Vonn spoke.

"This is what we're gonna do," I said. "Call BNE and let him know what happened to Con-Artist. After that, tell him you got the ups on one of them niggas and you want him to ride with you. He gone show up because he ain't gonna wanna look like he was on some hoe shit. Then you call Rone and tell him we got his cut from that lick. Tell him to meet us at that park over them projects by TNT house. When we get there, we gone smoke him and BNE at the same time. Both of them fuck niggas need to be dealt with and they both gone get it…Tonight!"

Vonn nodded his head, picked up his phone, and put the play in motion. He had blood in his eyes and tonight he was going to get it.

Chapter 11

It took me and Vonn a little over twenty minutes to make it to the park. We drove out there separately, so once we made it, Vonn hopped out of his wheels and jumped in my passenger seat. By the time he laid the seat back and got comfortable, I already had that good reef blowing through the air.

"What now?" Vonn questioned.

"Now we wait," 'I calmly answered.

We had been passing the blunt back and forth for fifteen minutes, before a pair of bright headlights pulled into a parking lot beside us.

"That looks like BNE right there," Vonn stated.

"Tell jit to hop in," I instructed.

Vonn rolled his window down and waved BNE over when he stepped out of his car. When BNE stepped over to the car and pulled on the door handle on the back passenger side, it was locked. I hit the automatic unlock button on my door and when BNE heard the click sound, he pulled the door open and eased his way in.

"What's good y'all? What the play is?" BNE spoke.

"You got your phone on you?" Vonn asked him and ignored his question.

"Yeah, I got it, what's up?"

"My shit died on me. Let me see you shit real quick to call this nigga."

BNE gave Vonn his phone and then sat back without a second thought.

Vonn quickly dialed a number and then placed BNE's phone to his ear.

"Aye, where you at?" Vonn spoke into the phone. After receiving his answer, he said, "Alright…well hurry up, nigga, we already here. My shit had died, this bra number…Alright, cool."

Vonn disconnected the call and handed BNE his phone back. "He on his way," Vonn spoke.

"Who was that?" BNE questioned.

"That nigga Rone," Vonn answered.

"Is he sliding with us too?"

"Fuck no! He's the one getting slid!"

"Damn, I thought Rone was straight?"

"Ain't nobody straight when you go against the grain,0" Vann barked.

"Say less," BNE started while looking out of his window.

We sat in silence for about twenty minutes before Vonn finally spoke and said, "Man, where the fuck this nigga at? Let me see your phone again, BNE."

BNE handed over his phone for the second time and Vonn called Rone again. The phone rang about five times and then Rone's voice came on the line, but it was his voicemail. Vonn hung up and called again, but this time the call went straight to voicemail. He tried one more time and got the same results.

"You think he suspects something?" Vonn asked me.

"I don't know, but something's definitely up," I answered honestly.

I looked around and started getting an awkward feeling that I should leave.

"Fuck it, let's burn up and catch that nigga another day. We can't get the two for one, but we can still get one though," I stated to Vonn.

Vonn cocked the slide back on his Glock and when I glanced at him, I saw a tear slide down his face. This was probably going to be hard for him, but fuck all that, it had to be done.

"Go ahead and holla at ya lil dawg for a minute and then I'll catch up with you tomorrow," I spoke to Vonn, basically urging him on.

"Alright, big bra, I'll get at you tomorrow," Von spoke while exiting the car.

"Stay up, big bra," BNE said to me while also making his exit.

I crunk my engine up and didn't respond. I don't understand snitchanese.

By the time BNE closed the door behind him and turned around to face Vonn, Vonn had already been locked and loaded and waiting on him to turn around.

"Whoa! What the fuck you doing, bra?" BNE yelled in disbelief and threw his hands up.

"We supposed to be brothers, bra. How the fuck could you turn on the fam?" Vonn gritted through his tears.

"What the fuck you mean, bra, what the fuck?"

I rolled the window down on my passenger side and blurted out. "Aye! Vonn, cut the bullshit, bra. We ain't got time for all that theatrical fuck shit! This ain't no fucking movie, nigga! Smoke his fucking boots and get off the scene!"

"Hold up, bra, I promise I—"

Boom! Boom!

BNE's head snapped back, and his body crashed into the side of my rental.

"What the fuck, nigga!" I blurted at Vonn.

"Say no more, big bra, it's handled," Vonn blurted back.

"Nigga you should've handled that shit over there!" I blurted while pointing towards car. "You done got this nigga sour ass blood all on the side of my shit! This a sucka free ride, nigga!"

Vonn just looked at me like I was crazy.

I smiled and said, "Lighten up, lil bra. Don't lose no sleep over a rat."

I rolled the window back up and calmly drove away while thinking about why that nigga Rone was a no-show.

Twenty minutes later, I pulled into the lot of a gas station off Bouldercrest Road and when I parked, I realized I was at the Texaco one of my all-time favorite rappers used to always rap about. *Gucci Mane.*

That nigga made this same Texaco famous. Guwop wasn't really making no noise these days on the rap tip, but back when I was a young nigga running the street of Orlando back in 08-09, Guwop had the streets on smash and his music played a major role in a lot of my back in the day bullshit.

Good Times.

I really parked here to contemplate where I should go though. I'd like to slide through Justice's spot, but I damn sho wasn't tryna be there if the police showed up, asking questions about that hoe brother.

I'd also like to pick up where I had left off with Dora, but it was way too late, so I'm damn near positive that hoe was asleep right now. That really only left Tori, but after seeing myself in those surveillance photos taken by the DEA, her spot made me nervous.

Even though it wasn't about me, my own situation that got me here was deeper than rap and beyond comprehension. Slippers count and I don't plan on slipping.

With that in mind, my best bet was actually Dora's spot, so my new plan was simple. Get all of my shit from Tori's house and take everything to her best friend's house.

Fuck it.

Tori wouldn't be happy about my sudden departure, but oh well. This wasn't about her…it was about me. Even though I do got feelings for that bitch now, they only way I could see it working out with her at this point was if she were willing to drop everything she had and move away. And even that was still risky.

The moment I put the car in drive and looked up, my eyes locked in on a gorgeous redbone posted up by the bus stop known as *the 32 Bouldercrest.* I immediately looked at my watch to view what time it was, 12:42 a.m.

I brought my car around and pulled up on her with my passenger window down. "Kind of late to be waiting on the bus, ain't it?" I asked with a grin.

The redbone bent her head down and peeked inside my ride. Her eyes roamed over my appearance and then they checked out the inside of my car. She cautiously took a step closer and rested her hands on the bottom of the open window frame.

"Hey," she shyly spoke. "Yeah, it's late and I'm sure the bus ain't coming but unfortunately, my phone is dead so hoping for this bus is my only option."

"So right now, you're just standing there looking all dolled up and hoping for a bus you know ain't coming?" I questioned with a smirk.

"It sounds kind of crazy when you put it like that, but I guess."

"Well, from the outside looking in, it looks like you're standing at a currently vacant bus stop and probably selling pussy."

She stood back up with her hands on her wide hips and said, "You gone seriously try me like that?"

"Since you can't deny it, I'll take that as confirmation. Get in the car."

Redbone looked around one more time, looked at my car, and then opened the passenger door. She took a seat and kept her hands in her lap with a weird look on her face.

She then turned to me and said, "You know there's a really weird mess on the side of your car?"

"What does it look like?"

"Looks like somebody threw ketchup all over the side of your car."

"I got one of them psycho baby mamas," I stated.

I looked at her with a stern gaze and she nervously wiggled under my stare. I reached into my pocket and pulled out a one-hundred-dollar bill. I waved the bill around and then handed it to her.

I don't know who this pretty bitch thinks she is fooling, but it damn sho ain't me.

She quietly took the money just like I knew she would and then told me to drive down the street and pull into the Sun Valley Apartments.

"Sun Valley?" I questioned. "You tryna set a nigga up or something? Just cause I ain't from round here don't mean I'm green, baby."

"It ain't nothing like that. That's where I live…I'm just giving us a place to go."

I made a circle and pulled right back into the Texaco. I parked on the side of the building and threw my seat back. I rolled up, fired up the blunt, and took a deep pull, while my new passenger kept her eyes locked on me with interest.

When I finally spoke, I said, "We good right here. I'm straight on the pussy anyway…I just wanna see what that mouth does."

I unbuckled my Gucci belt, pulled my pants and boxers down to my thighs and leaned back, but not too far back. I made sure I was elevated enough to still keep an eye on my surroundings. I had a lot on my mind, a lot had just happened, and some good random head from the pretty bitch was just what the doctor ordered.

Redbone looked at me like she couldn't believe I ain't have no interest in getting between her thick ass thighs.

"You sure you don't wanna get a room or something? I promise you'll get your money's worth," she purred.

"I ain't tryna hear yo mouth, I'm tryna feel yo mouth. Less talking, more action. Tighten up before I take my money back and kick you out my shit."

I took another pull of my blunt and redbone quickly dropped her face into my lap. She took my soft dick into her warm mouth and slurped me to attention.

Once I was hard and tall, she released me from her lips and scowl stroked my length while saying, "Damn, baby."

"What I told you about talking?" I stated and pushed her head back down.

I swatted her hand away from my pole and used both of my hands to pull her hair up into a ponytail. I lifted my hips up, and she made a loud gagging noise as my dick slipped past her tonsils. I then firmly held her head in place and pounded my dick into her throat like I was stabbing her in the mouth,

To my surprise, she didn't choke or run from the dick. I let her head go and she immediately went to work on her own. She had so much spit leaking from her mouth, it was soaking my thighs. The minute she noticed the mess she was creating, she pulled me out of her mouth and began licking all the spit up from my thighs and balls. She sucked both of my balls into her mouth and began licking all the spit up from my thighs and balls. She sucked both of my balls into her mouth and stroked my dick at the same time, while looking at me.

Usually, I don't even like getting my balls licked from this angle because they hang down between my legs and that makes me feel like her mouth to be too close to my ass. Some of these bitches out here freaky as fuck, and even though I'ma Scorpio and a bonafide freak my damn self, I ain't that damn freaky.

I reluctantly let her do her thing though and just kept my eyes on the bitch.

She then lifted her head and put me back into her throat until her lips touched my body and then sucked me from tip to base repeatedly in a smooth motion.

This bitch was sucking me up like a damn porn star. Her slurp sounds and her constant moaning with my dick in her throat finally got to me and I exploded into her mouth. The moment she felt my first stream of nut spray into her throat, she pulled her head back, and my next two streams splashed her on the face.

She rubbed my dick around her face and all over her lips while still moaning and looking me in my eyes. She then placed two kisses on my dick head, sucked me one more time to make sure I was clean and drained, and then finally released me and sat up. She wiped her mouth and stared at me.

All I could think was, damn!

Now this bitch had me thinking about getting that room she requested, because after that performance I ain't have no doubt, I would indeed get my money's worth. But fuck all that, I had places to go and people to see.

"Bet that up, Red," I lazily said.

"You're welcome, daddy. That dick tastes good too, baby. Can I get some? Please? I don't even want no more money…Hell, you can get this money you gave me back! I just wanna sit on that long ass dick, baby…Please."

Damn, this bitch was driving a hard bargain.

I thought about it for a moment then said, "That sounds good and all, but I'm straight. Get out."

She looked at me with one of them lil girl pouts and poked her bottom lip out.

I looked at her like, *what the fuck you waiting on?*

She eventually got the picture and made her exit. I watched her wide ass cheeks jiggle away and strut back over to the bus stop where she resumed her nightly post. The nasty bitch didn't even wipe her face off.

I pulled away from the Texaco and made my way to Tori's house.

Chapter 12

When I pulled into the driveway at Tori's house, the first thing I did was drag a water hose from the side of the house and spray down the side of my rental. I would have completely ignored the BNE residue, if the lil freak hoe hadn't said something about it. Yeah, I probably looked kind of flaky standing there hosing down my car at 2:30 in the morning but fuck it. I'd slide through a car wash and then swap it out later on, but this would have to do for now.

Once that was over, I headed straight for the shower and cleaned myself up. Tori was still knocked out and lightly snoring when I stepped out of the shower, so I decided to use that time to pack my shit.

I still had a bag full of drugs and money and my second bag was still filled to the brim with hundreds. The only thing I really had less of from when I first arrived was bricks. Other than that, my bank was still sitting pretty, and I now had a closet full of clothes and shit.

I packed my clothes up and took all of my shoe boxes to the car. I put all of my jewelry in a bag and took that and my two duffle bags to the car as well. Anything else was minor and not needed.

It was almost five in the morning when I got through with that and I was now officially tired. I flopped into the bed with Tori not caring if I woke her up or not, and then passed out the minute I was warmly under the covers.

***

I snapped back to reality later on to the smell of bacon and eggs. Tori was standing over me with a plateful of food and a big ass smile on her face.

Tori handed me the plate and said, "Good morning, bae."

"What time is it?" I asked while instantly diggin in.

"It's about to be noon," she replied while crawling in the bed next to me.

I swallowed a mouthful of bacon, eggs, and toast and said, "So what's on yo agenda today?"

"I go to work at two o'clock. Until then, nothing."

While chewing more food, I contemplated telling her I'd be leaving today but decided against it. It'll probably be better if I just took off while she was at work. Then I wouldn't have to deal with her mouth.

Tori sat there with me for the next twenty minutes and watched me eat.

"You know I love you, right?" Tori blurted out of nowhere.

I looked at her and immediately started feeling kind of bad. It figures she would throw some shit like that at a nigga while a nigga was plotting on hauling ass. I definitely didn't want to say it back though, so I played it smooth.

I put the empty plate on the dresser beside me and said, "Show me how much you love me."

I was already laying in my boxers and her hands has been rubbing all over me the whole time I was eating anyway, so I knew she was waiting on me to finish eating so she could jump on me. She wanted to feed me and fuck me.

She climbed on top of me and kissed me on my lips. Our mouths parted and out tongues began twirling together. She was still wearing one of her usual nightgowns, so I lifted it up and got two big handfuls of ass. While messaging her cheeks she rubbed on my chest and used her long red nails to lightly scratch me. She moved down and planted her lips on my chest. She used her tongue to taste along my many tattoos while continuing to work her way down.

When she reached my waist, she yanked my boxers down and my dick bounced out like a diving board. She gripped my dick at the base and waved it in her face. She then stuck her tongue out and began licking my pole like a popsicle.

I threw my hands behind my head and watched her do her thing. She started out sucking on my dick head and then slowly eased her way down. I felt my tip hit the back of her throat and heard her gag. Her eyes teared up but to my surprise, she opened her mouth wider and kept pushing. Her mouth eventually made contact with my body and then she looked up at me.

She had just swallowed my entire dick for the first time, and I couldn't believe it.

"That's what I'm talkin bout, baby. Get that dick right," I coached while enjoying the show.

She pulled her head up and then bounced her face in my lap. She worked me over with her mouth from top to bottom. Every time, she got to my tip, she would lick her tongue all around it and make a loud slurping sound, before going back down.

My dick started jumping and throbbing in her throat and she knew I was on the verge of filling her mouth with nut. Instead of letting me nut, she squeezed my dick with her hands and pulled me out of her mouth.

She stroked me up and down with both hands and then climbed on top of me. She rubbed my tip along her slit and then slowly eased herself down on me. Once all the way down, she came instantly and gushed all over me.

"I ain't never had no dick this good," Tori moaned while shaking.

She then leaned forward with her hands on my chest and turned up. She started popping her pussy and bouncing her ass like she was listening to a Megan Thee Stallion song. She galloped on me like she was riding a horse and in no time, I felt her juices raining down on me again.

She tooted her ass up, arched her back, looked back at me and said, "Beat this pussy, baby!"

I pushed my head into her opening and dug my length into her in one push.

"Shit, bae! Wait!" Tori shouted and held one hand out to try and push me back.

"Ain't no wait! This is what you wanted!" I barked while pulling back. I slapped her on both cheeks and said, "Now shut up and take this dick!"

I pushed back into her, and her ass bounced and jiggled against my body. I gripped her waits firmly and beat that pussy up with straight deep hard and long strokes.

"Ahh, shit! Wait! Fuck! Shit! Damn!" Tori shouted after every stroke.

"Squirt on this dick, baby!" I ordered. "You wanna squirt after every stroke?"

"Fuck! Fuck! Fuck! Fu-Fu-Fu-Fuck! Shit! Shit!"

"Answer the question!" I shouted and slapped the ass while still drilling the pussy.

"Yes! Yes! Ye-Yessss!"

"Well, what are you waiting for?"

"I'm-I-I'm cumming, baby! I'm cummming!"

Right on cue, I looked down and watched Tori squirt all over my dick. Her juices leaked onto the bed and created a puddle. I maintained my rough assault on her pussy while her body was shaking and eventually, I sprayed her walls with my nut.

I fell on top of her and kept grinding into her plump booty until I was sure all of my nuts had been drained. I then planted a kiss on the back of her neck and rolled off of her.

"Damn, that pussy good," I blurted.

"I can't breathe," Tori moaned. "You tried to kill me," she added.

I laughed and slapped her on her soft volleyball-shaped booty.

"Ouch!" Tori shrieked with her face still burned into the bed. She still hadn't moved from her position.

I looked at the clock on the dresser and said "Oh, shit! It's damn near 1:30, bae! You gotta get yo ass to work!"

"I'm calling off," she groaned.

"Why the fuck would you do that?"

"Because I can't move. I'll never make it."

"Stop playing and go hop your ass in the shower," I stated and slapped her on the ass again.

"Ouch, bae! Damn!"

I slapped that ass again.

"Ouch! Okay! Shit! Just give me a minute."

I shrugged my shoulders and rolled out of the bed. I needed to shower my damn self and then figure out how my day would go. I definitely needed to contact Dora and find out if she'd let me slide over and lay up in her shit for a while.

Tori would be heartbroken, so telling her where I was going wasn't an option. I could just get a hotel, but then I'd be holed up with no purpose. At least being laid up with Dora would give me some type of balance. I needed that. Being on the run ain't always easy.

While I was stepping out of Tori's shower, she had finally moved off the bed and was now taking my place in the shower. Her shower was quick and after dressing, she flew out the house. She was definitely going to be late.

I whipped my phone out and called Dora. She didn't answer, so I sent her a quick text and told her to hit me up as soon as she got a chance.

She quickly texted me back and let me know she was working. I told her a situation came up and I needed to come over first chance she's got. She told me to meet her at her waitress job and she would give me her house keys.

While texting back and forth with her, my phone started ringing and it was Vonn.

"What's up, bra!" I answered.

"You're at my sister's house, right?"

"Open the door, I'm outside."

I hung up the phone and walked to the front door. I unlocked the door and sure enough, Vonn was standing on the other side.

"What's up, lil bra?" I spoke while stepping aside to let him in.

"This shit keeps getting wilder and wilder, big bra," Vonn stated while flopping down on the couch.

"Talk to me," I stated while joining him in the living room.

"Man, CNN got locked up this morning. They got bra booked for two counts of first-degree murders."

"Oh, shit! What the fuck happened?"

"He found out where one of them Riverdale niggas stayed at and pulled up. The nigga was standing in front of his house with two other niggas, and bra let all them niggas have it! The one that didn't get hit knew who bra was and put the police on bra. Them crackas picked him up this morning at his baby mama house."

"So, how many of them niggas is it?" I questioned.

"It's like five more of them niggas...six, including Rone."

"Damn," I mumbled. "You lil bad ass jits got me caught up in the middle of all this fuck shit! Y'all 'posed to be out here getting money, but how the fuck y'all gone do that with all this beef? You need to handle that shit!"

"Trust me, big bra, we gone smoke all them niggas!!" Vonn declared.

"I need to slide through TNT spot for a minute and after that, I'ma pull up on YFN. that's 'bout all I got planned for the day I'll probably be in the house tonight."

"Alright…well, I'm about to slide to a car wash then swap my rental out. Oh yeah, I gotta drop my shit off before I swap out. Shit getting too hot over here and I ain't tryna bring on heat on yo sister while all this shit going down, so I'm ducking off somewhere else."

"Alright…well, I'll link up with you later on after I link up with the gang," Vonn stated while rising from the couch.

We walked out of the house together and hopped into our separate whips. I pulled out behind him and decided it would be better if I grabbed the keys from Dora first, since her job was the closest out of the neighborhood and we headed in the same direction. I pulled up right behind him at a red light and picked up my phone to send a quick text, letting Dora know I was on my way.

Tat! Tat! Tat! Tat! Tat! Tat! Tat!

Bang! Bang! Bang! Boom!

"Oh, shit!" I blurted while reaching for my pistol.

When the gunfire first erupted, my initial reaction was to duck down, but once I realized the gunshots were not being aimed in my direction, I quickly popped back up with my cannon in hand. It was at that very moment I realized the gunshots had been aimed at Vonn.

"Oh shit!" I blurted again while jumping out of my car.

The light turned green and the all-black Yukon that had just unloaded on Vonn immediately screeched off. I let off a couple of shots and shattered the Yukon's back window, but in a matter of seconds the truck was out of sight.

I quickly ran over to Vonn's car while hoping the bra was straight. When I looked inside of his window, he leaned over his steering wheel with blood dripping down his face.

"Fuck!" I gritted.

I opened his door and pulled him out of the car. He fell to the ground and then surprised me by opening his eyes and slowly getting up. "What the fuck!" I shouted. "You playing possum, nigga?"

He looked at me in a daze and did not respond. I helped him to his feet and leaned him against the car. I quickly looked him up and down and the only blood leakage I could see coming from a gash on his face, but he didn't appear to be shot.

"You straight?" I questioned.

"I feel like I just got hit upside the head with a brick," Vonn mumbled.

I quickly looked inside his car and saw a big ass piece of glass laying across the center console. The whole passenger side had holes in it and both windows on the passenger side were shattered.

"I think you just got hit in the face with a piece of glass when the window shattered," I informed him. "You should be straight."

"Yeah, I'm good," Vonn stated more coherently,

Sirens started sounding off in the distance around us.

"Fuck!" I blurted. "Get in my car!" I ordered.

We scrambled back to my rental, and I quickly mashed the gas and swerved around Vonn's shot-up car.

"What I'm posed to do about the car?" Vonn asked.

"Fuck that car!" I answered. "Leave that shit right there and worry about that shit later! Right now, we need to get you off the scene."

Chapter 13

I took Vonn to TNT's house, since that was his original destination anyway. Plus, his house would probably be crawling with police in no time because of the shot-up rental car that was in Nina Alina's name. When we pulled up, TNT was standing in his driveway, along with SUN and NUT.

SUN was the first person to notice the blood and anxiety on Vonn's face and blurted, "Oh shit! What's up, NV? What the fuck? Are you straight?

"Yeah, I'm good," Vonn replied.

"Damn, yo! What the fuck happened to yo face, son?" NUT spoke with his northern accent up high.

"Them Riverdale niggas caught me slippin and tried to do me at a red light. Them fuck niggas swizz-cheesed my shit!"

"Take yo ass inside and get yourself right," TNT spoke.

Vonn walked straight into the house and disappeared beyond the doorway. I decide to sit on the trunk of my car and roll up a blunt. A nigga nerves stay on high around this bitch. I done been through way too much. I left my own bullshit miles away, just to end up right in the middle of some more shit.

SUN rolled up to match my blunt and the four of us got a rotation going.

"You lil niggas need to get y'all shit together," I spoke to the crowd while exhaling a cloud of smoke.

"We need to stock up on some sticks," TNT commented.

"Y'all need to stack up on some bodies!" I blurted.

While passing the blunt to my right, I peeped a dark green Malibu LT rolling down the block, and something about it immediately raised my antennas. I instinctively reached for my cannon and held it firmly.

"Y'all niggas know that car?" I asked the group.

Everybody looked at the car that was approaching at a normal pace, but nobody spoke.

Eventually SUN spoke up and said, "Ain't nobody in the car but a white bitch, and everybody knows how I feel about them bunnies."

SUN stepped to the road and waited for the car to approach that was indeed being driven by a snowflake. The car didn't have any tint and all of the windows were down. I let my guard down a little and eased up, while taking one of the blunts that was still in rotation.

SUN then stepped into the road and got in front of the car. He began waving his hands and signaling for the snow bunny to pull over. When the bunny was about ten feet away, she suddenly slammed on the gas and her Malibu quickly lurched forward and slammed into SUN with a loud smack. SUN fell to the ground and the bitch ran him over like he was a speed bump.

"Yo, what the fuck?" NUT shouted.

While SUN was being used as a speed bump, a group of niggas wearing ski masks popped up from their ducked-down positions inside the car and immediately started letting off shots.

With my pistol still in hand, I quickly burst back and dove to the side. I rolled up on one knee beside my car and emptied my clip into the Malibu.

Gunshots were erupting all around me and everybody appeared to be putting in work.

One of the niggas hanging out of the window of the Malibu took a face shot and fell out of the car onto the street. The Malibu then screeched away and left tire marks in the middle of the street.

The nigga that fell out of the car was laying faceless in the road next to SUN's lifeless body. I looked to my right and saw NUT laid out on the front lawn with blood seeping through his shirt.

TNT quickly dashed over to NUT screaming, "NUT! NUT!"

Vonn came running out of the house with his pistol in hand looking around like a crazed animal. The moment his eyes moved in the direction of NUT and TNT, he screamed.

"We gotta get him to a hospital!" TNT shouted. "Help me get him in a car!"

TNT grabbed NUT under his arms and Vonn grabbed his legs. Together they lifted him up and carried his body to TNT's car.

NUT coughed up blood while being pushed into the car and groaned, "Yo! Make sure y'all get them niggas, yo!"

“Just chill, NUT, we gone get you to a hospital! Just keep breathing!” TNT barked.

NUT coughed up more blood and groaned. “Yo…I ain’t gone make it, son.”

TNT jumped in his driver's seat without answering and shouted at Vonn, “Come on, bra, hurry up! Let’s ride!”

I quickly grabbed Vonn’s shoulder and shook my head.

I looked at TNT and said, “Get bra to the hospital and we’ll catch up with you later. Me and Vonn gone spin the block.”

“Say less,” TNT stated while zooming off.

“Let’s go," I stated to Vonn while quickly stepping into my rental.

As soon as Vonn sat his ass in the seat I pulled off.

“Call that nigga Rone,” I ordered. “Tell that nigga he either link up with us to get his cut from that lick right now, or he ain’t getting shit!”

Vonn quickly made the call and got on the line.

“What’s up, nigga!” Vonn blurted aggressively.

I quickly whispered, “Calm down, jit! Don’t scare the nigga.”

“Aye, I just called to let you know I’m riding with big bra, but bra about to head out of town, and you already know shit getting hot for me and my niggas right now, so I’m about to duck off for a while until shit die down. With that being said, me and bra still got yo cut from that lick the other night and if you want it, it’s now or never. We can either link up right now, or me and big bra gone bust yo shirt down.”

Vonn sat quiet for a couple of minutes while listening to whatever Rone had to say, then said, “Alright, we on the way now.”

Vonn hung up to the phone and said to me, “Slide over to the Burger King where we hit that sack on the lil geek jit. Rone gone meet us in the lot.”

I quickly made a U-turn and hi the gas towards our new destination. I took my Glock-17 off my waistline and tossed it in Vonn’s lap.

“Grab that box of bullets out of the glove compartment and load me back up, lil bra.”

Vonn did as I instructed and said, "So, what we about to do with Rone?"

"We finna snatch that fuck nigga up!" I blurted. "It ain't no damn coincidence them niggas keep pulling up at all y'all spots! One plus one equal two, lil bra. That nigga setting y'all up! More than half yo clique just disappeared in less than a week, nigga! FN gone, BNE gone Con-Artist gone, CNN fucked up, but I respect the way he went out. SUN gone, Nut might be gone, and you could've been gone! You better wake the fuck up! This shit dead serious, nigga! Them niggas smoke y'all ass right now! It's time to turn the tables around, and I'ma show you how to do it!"

Vonn just kept loading my Glock and didn't respond.

What could he say?

He gave me back my Glock and didn't respond as we were turning into the Burger King lot. I parked on the side in the cut and rolled up a blunt. Right before I sparked the blunt, Vonn's phone rang. He quickly answered and let Rone know we were parking in the cut.

As soon as Rone pulled up beside us, I hopped out of the car and Vonn followed suit. I was tired of playing around with these lil niggas. I tried to play the back field, but these niggas clearly weren't ready for the type of pressure they were in, so it was time to get fully involved. At this point, they really ain't leave me no choice.

Rone hopped out of an all-white Chevy Avalanche and pulled up on Vonn.

"What's good?" Rone said while dapping Vonn up. "I don't think y'all got away with anything. I heard the lick went a little sour."

"Shut yo bitch ass up!" I shouted and quickly slapped him over the head with the barrel of my Glock.

"Ahh, fuck!" Rone shrieked.

"I said shut up!" I barked and bashed his head two more times.

Rone quickly tumbled to the ground.

Whap! Whap! Whap!

I continued to fuck him up, with my anger consistently rising with each smirk

"Chill out, big bra! You gone kill him!" Vonn shouted.

"So what, nigga! These people better mind their fucking business!" I shouted. "Get yo bitch ass up!" I barked at Rone, while picking him up by his shirt collar.

As soon as he was on his feet, I pushed him towards my car and shoved him into the backseat. I still had my duffles and a couple shoe boxes in the backseat because I hadn't had the chance to take my shit to Dora's house, but most of my shit was in the trunk, so there was just enough room for Rone.

Despite the lack of space, I pushed him in deeper and climbed in next to him. I kept my Glock pressed up against his back and ordered Vonn to take the wheel and pull off. Vonn quickly took the helm and peeled out of the lot.

"What the fuck?" Rone cried. "I ain't got nothing to do with tha lick going sour! I promise!"

Wham!

I slammed the butt of my cannon into the back of Rone's skull and gave him another gash.

"Open yo bitch ass mouth again and I'm about to put yo brains on the dashboard!" I barked.

"Where are we going now?" Vonn questioned while weaving through traffic.

"Good question," I replied, "it's time to change the scoreboard." I looked at Tone and said, "When I ask you a question, you answer my question, got it?"

Rone shook his head up and down.

"I can't hear you!" I barked.

"Yes!" Rone shouted.

Wham!

"Who the fuck you yelling at?" I barked after delivering another blow to his skull.

I pushed his head between the two front seats and had him pinned against the center console.

I kept my Glock on his back and barked, "We bout to start pulling up on these bitch ass niggas, and you gone be the one to get us there…Got it?"

“Yeah,” Rone fearfully answered in a humble tone.

“Good! Now where these niggas hang at the most?” I questioned.

Rone blurted out a neighborhood I had never heard of before, so I had to ask, “And where the fuck is that?”

“It's in Riverdale,” Rone replied.

“Alright…well, sit back and enjoy the ride then,” I stated while making myself comfortable. “Let's get this show on the road,” I said to Vonn.

Say less,” Vonn replied.

Chapter 14

We pulled into the neighborhood that Rone directed us to, and slowly made our way to the house where a couple of oops were supposed to be hang out. I kept Rone's bitch ass pinned to the center console for the entire ride, while smoking the blunt I had rolled up before we abducted his bitch ass. He had to be uncomfortable because the ride wasn't short.

Before the ride, I had decided to pat the nigga down and came up on a Glock-19 with a thirty-round clip, fully loaded. I took that, and I also took his phone and some chump change.

"Alright, we are on the street now," I spoke to Rone. "Which house is it?"

"Fifth house on the left. All white," Rone replied.

As we crept up to the house, I noticed that nobody was outside.

"Call em," I ordered Rone and pushed his phone into his hand.

Rone quickly scrolled through his contact and made the call to the owner of the house.

When the recipient answered, Rone said, "Aye, where y'all at? I need to holla at y'all."

"Put it on speaker," I whispered.

Rone complied and then I heard a male's voice blurt through the phone, "I'm at the house with my lady, bra, I don't know where them niggas at."

"Tell him to come outside," I firmly whispered.

"Alright…well, come outside real quick so I can run some shit by you before I pull off. I'm already outside," Rone spoke.

I then snatched the phone back and hung up.

"Keep yo bitch ass down and don't move," I ordered.

Within two minutes, they came out the front door hand-in-hand, and I instantly recognized her as the red bitch CNN had knocked out in the club that night.

This must be the nigga that hit bra with the bottle.

"Air them out," I stated to Vonn.

Vonn quickly jumped out of the car and let his Nina bark until the tall nigga and the red bitch were both sprawled out in their driveway. He then quickly slid back into the car and hit the gas.

"Next," I said to Rone.

"I got to make a call to find out where the boys were. You heard bra tell me he didn't know where everybody at," Rone spoke.

"Me and the gang at my spot right now, waiting on the plug to pull up and drop this work off. Pull up, nigga," the deep voice spoke.

"Ask him who is all there," I whispered.

"Who are you all with?" Rone asked.

"Everybody but LJ and DJ. DJ got popped earlier on a mission. We pulled up on them niggas in the A earlier and bra ain't make it."

"Yeah, that's what I wanna holla at y'all 'bout. I got some info on the nigga NV I know y'all gone wanna hear."

"Mannn, we smashed that nigga NV earlier at a red light. That pussy nigga was tryna hide with his face in his lap." The deep voice laughed.

I looked at Vonn and could see his face balled up with anger.

"He didn't die," Rone informed. "Y'all didn't hit him at all actually. The nigga just called me and he wanna meet up. We can trap him up later on tonight."

"Just swing by. We'll talk about it when you pull up."

"Cool," Rone stated before ending the call.

I snatched the phone back and patted Rone on his back. "Good job." I laughed.

"Them fuck niggas got me fucked up!" Vonn shouted while switching lanes.

"Ease up, soldier, ease-ease…we gon get 'em…we gone have fun tonight." I looked at Rone and asked, "So how many niggas over there?"

"Four," Rone replied.

"And we might get lucky and catch them plugged at the same time. We need a redo on that anyway...oh yeah, we 'bout to put some work in tonight!" I stated.

I kicked back and started thinking about how I could make the work, while Rone directed Vonn to our next destination.

PART 2

BO-T

Chapter 15

I woke up in the back seat of the Jaguar and listened to the rain bounce off the roof. My whole body was on fire but fuck it, I was built under pressure, I could endure the pain. I leaned over and grabbed the bottle of Tylenol I had on the floor and popped the lid, threw back three of them and swallowed them with my spit. I laid my head back down and watched the rain fall down the window, while thinking about a better place to lay my head. Anywhere had to be better than in the back seat of a stolen, dead federal agent's Jaguar, parked in an alley behind an abandoned warehouse.

After dropping Wizz off at the hospital, I sped off and didn't look back. It hurt me to leave my nigga behind like that but I really ain't have a choice. I couldn't just sit back and watch my nigga die and the hospital seemed like his only hope for survival.

My own injuries were bad, but not as bad as I thought. Turns out my worst injury was a dislocated shoulder. It originally looked like my arm was broken, but I was double jointed, so my shit just naturally looked crazy. My shoulder had popped out of place though and made my whole arm inoperable. I had cuts and gashes all over my face and body. Bruises from top to bottom and lot of blood on me that mainly belonged to Wizz.

I didn't know where the fuck I was at or where I was going, but I drove like I had it all figured out. I ended up pulling into a corner store in hopes of finding someone to go in the store and buy me some pain pills, but by the time I stopped the car I could barely move.

I managed to roll the window down when a big, athleletic-looking black kid walked by and got his attention. My appearance scared the nigga at first, but his fear quickly turned into concern, and he slowly approached me. He's the one that realized my shoulder was dislocated. He was a high school football player and had had a dislocated shoulder before, so the swelling and irregular size of my shoulder instantly told him what was wrong.

He offered to pop my arm back in place and did so while I bit down on my seat belt. He went inside the store and bought me two bottles of Tylenol and a couple bottles of water. I gave the young nigga a blue face, and he kept it moving without ever questioning me,

I then drove off and eventually made my way into the alley I was in now behind the empty warehouse. I've been parked back here for five days straight and had not moved yet. I haven't eaten anything or drink anything after knocking off the last water bottle, I had. The daily and nightly pain constantly surging through my body had almost gotten the best of me. I felt like I was in Vietnam or some shit. A soldier left to survive on his own.

Here I was now, five days straight and the pain was finally subsiding. The pain was still front and center, but it had gotten to a point where I felt as if I could finally move.

I sat up in the car and leaned against the seat, popped the lock up on the door and swung the door open. A bright bolt of lightning flashed through the dark sky and momentarily illuminated the surroundings. The sound of the pouring rain increased and appeared to be the only sound I could hear, and the thunder that followed behind the lightning.

I stepped out of the car and was immediately soaked and pelted by the rain. I slowly stripped butt naked and kicked all of my bloody attire to the side. I ain't had a shower in five days, and this was as good as it was going to get for the moment. I mainly wanted to let the rain cleanse me of the built-up dirt, sweat, blood and tears that has stained my body over the last few days.

I tried to stretch and nearly threw up. My stomach was tight and empty. My body was weakbut I was determined to change that tonight.

Once I felt like the rain did the best it could do, I slid my soaking wet and naked body back in the backseat of my hot Jaguar. I reached for the keys under the seat and leaned over the center console to start the car. When the car came to life, I turned the heater on high and let the hot air dry my body.

The agent that once occupied this car had left a luggage bag full of clothes in the back seat, so once I was dry, I looked through the clothing items and selected some boxers, socks, gym shorts, and a polo shirt that damn near choked me. The one pair of shoes in the bag didn't fit but he had a pair of no-name flip flops that fit just fine.

I cringed while climbing over the center console and then eased myself into the driver's seat. I leaned over and unzipped the duffle bag sitting in the passenger seat. I had one more duffle on the floor in the front of the passenger seat, and one on the floor in the back underneath the luggage bag that had the agent's clothes.

I removed a pair of blue faces from the duffle bag and then unzipped my treasure chest.

Where the fuck do I go now?

I put the car in drive and decided that my first destination needed to be somewhere I could fill my belly. I slowly pulled in front of the warehouse and eventually made my way onto the main road. The clock on the dashboard read 10:38 p.m., so that limited my options.

The very first food joint that I crossed paths with was a Wendy's and I damn near crashed while swerving into their parking lot. I hit the drive-thru line and pulled up to the speaker box.

"Welcome to Wendy's, how may I help you?" a female spoke through the speaker.

"Let me get one of everything on the menu and two large Sprites," I answered.

The lady didn't respond.

"You heard me? I said, let me get one of everything on the menu and two large Sprites," I spoke louder.

"Is this a prank?" the woman asked.

I was instantly agitated. "Does it sound like a prank, bitch! Who the fuck got time to be playing at this time of night? You talking to a grown ass, hungry ass nigga with a bag, bitch! The fuck I look like pulling a prank in a Wendy's drive-thru line? Give me one of everything on your cheap ass menu and shut up!"

"Ummm...wow...okay. The attitude is very unnecessary but okay, one of everything for the grown ass, hungry ass nigga with a bag coming up," the lady sarcastically spoke.

She took a moment to ring up my order and then told me my total. I pulled up to the window and was immediately blown away by the young, pretty ass black chick waiting on me.

"For a nigga with a so-called bag, I damn sho can't tell! Grown and hungry? Yeah, I can go for that, but you pull up to my window in this dirty ass…what are you in, a Jaguar? Okay, you in a dirty ass Jaguar, you got on a shirt that's about to strangle yo thick ass neck, that must be ya lil brother shirt, and you look like a nigga that just got beat up and scratched all in the face by a mad ass cat! Nigga with a bag, my ass! Hurry up and pay for all this damn food!

"And who the fuck you supposed to be anyway? You made an order like you got two football teams riding with you and your big black blockhead ass pulled up to a bitch window by yourself, wearing yo lil brother shirt. Where they do that at?

I thought maybe you was a rapper or somebody coming through late night, but nigga you ain't shit! You just a nigga with a big ass neck and a tight ass shirt! Boy, bye! And why the fuck you just sitting there staring at a bitch? You gone pay for the damn food or is your ass really broke? Nigga, you…"

I raised my hand and she finally stopped talking. I had the wad of blue faces in my grasp and slowly peeled off three of them. My food didn't even come up to one-fifty, so I threw all three bills into the black girl's face and snapped.

"Keep the change, black ass bitch! Yo poor ass out here working in a damn Wendy's drive-thru line at eleven o'clock at night and got the nerve to try and run your fat black ass mouth! Bitch, yo big black ass lips look like they were made to wrap around my dick! I ain't gone lie, you pretty as fuck, but you so damn black, I can barely make out yo facial features! Bitch, you purple! You got the nerve to have yo hair done this cute to be working at Wendy's. Who you tryna to look cute for, the nigga shakin the fries?

"Burger flippin ass bitch! You are probably about six months pregnant in there with a flat ass booty! I wish I could see the rest of your body, so I could really ride your burnt black ass! Where is my food at, bitch? I ain't got no more rap for yo lil ghetto ass. Go separate the ketchup and mustard and earn yo living, hoe…get my shit."

"Yo ass probably gonna regret buying all of this shit just to look cool. You ain't impressing nobody! Take your muscle head ass to the next window and get your shit!" the black girl shouted and slammed her window.

I laughed at the bitch and pulled up to the next window. An older black lady rolled her eyes at me and handed me bags full of food, along with my two drinks. The aroma floating from the many different bags instantly filled the car and made my mouth water.

Fuck these bitches, I'm 'bout to fuck this food up!

I couldn't wait to dig in, so I quickly whipped the car into a parking spot on the side of the building and parked next to a black two-door Honda. I pushed my seat back as far as it would go with the two bags behind me and shut the car off. My shirt was definitely too tight, so I snatched it off over my head and put it in the back seat.

I poked through the bags and pondered over my wide variety of choices. I decided to ace the Baconator first with some fries, chicken nuggets and my Sprite. I popped three more Tylenols while I ate and filled my stomach to the max. I felt like I hadn't eaten in years!

Once I was full, I opened everything I hadn't touched yet and took a couple bites of everything, just to enjoy the taste. I ended up so full, I couldn't move.

I made sure my doors were locked and then I leaned the seat all the way back so I could be in a more comfortable position to digest my round-table meal. I closed my eyes and began thinking about what my next destination should be.

I needed to take a real shower and scrub my body with soap. I needed clothes that fit, and I needed shelter. To make matters even worse, I didn't even have a clue where I was at. That was going to be difficult. Before I knew it, my head was rolling to the side, and I was fast asleep.

Chapter 16

My eyes popped open, and I reflexively reached for my waistline. I didn't have a pistol on my hip, so the gesture was useless. I did have a fully loaded arsenal in the back seat though.

The tapping noise that pulled me from my sleep caught my attention again and when I looked up, the pretty purple bitch that allows the bullshit in the drive-thru window was tapping in my window and saying something I couldn't understand. She was pointing and laughing though, so I know she's with the bullshit.

I looked around and saw all of the empty food wrappers and half-eaten sandwiches all over the dashboard, so I knew this had to be a bad look. I probably looked like a hobo that had just pigged out at Wendy's, and then passed out in the damn parking lot.

The Wendy's hoe was still laughing and making faces at me that I could barely make out since it was dark outside. I looked at a time on the dashboard and saw that it was 2:11 a.m. My exhausted body had shut down on me around midnight, so I wasn't out long. I actually really needed the rest, and this bitch was once again getting on my nerves.

I unlocked my door and pushed it open.

"Yo homeless ass tryna hit a bitch with yo dirty ass door now? Nigga, I knew you wasn't shit! Look at you! You look pitiful! You out here riding around with your whole life in your back seat. Nigga, you trespassing right now. Ain't nobody told you that you could sleep here. Take yo black ass down the street to the shelter and get you a bed! Poor ass nigga! That money you had was your whole life savings and from the looks of it, your life ain't shit! I see you did yourself a favor and took off that tight shirt! You probably ate all the food and ripped it! You can get another one from the Salvation Army though. Just make sure you do yourself a favor and get a bigger size! Block head ass."

"Shut yo purple ass up, bitch! Burger-baggin ass hoe! Shouldn't you be chopping up pickles right now?" I snapped while swinging my legs out of the car and standing up.

Me and that bitch was the same height, five-eight, so we stood eye-to-eye. I stood right in her face, and she didn't back down. She put her hand on her hip and cocked her head to the side.

I looked her up and down and was actually surprised. I knew this black ass chick was pretty in the face, but damn! She turned out to be the total package in the looks department. Her thighs were thick and toned and her hips were soft and wide. Her waist was small, and her breasts were at least D-cups. For a bitch in a Wendy's uniform, she was definitely a jaw dropper.

While I was looking at her, she was looking at me, and even though I was is a rough state, I was still that nigga. Muscles still on point, arms bulging, chest poking out, abs rock hard. My gold teeth were gleaming in the night and my cut was only a week old, so it's still straight.

"Damn! Yo homeless ass built like a damn action figure," she joked.

"We can go back and forth with the bullshit all night if that's what you want, but in all honesty, I'm tired. I really need some sleep and I really need a whole lot of other shit and you might be able to help me."

"Help you?" She burst out laughing. "If you need help, yo ass better holla at the Red Cross! You got me fucked up! Nigga, you—"

"Ease up, baby! Ease! We got off on the wrong foot and I'll accept it's probably my fault. If you know what I had going on out here, you'd be surprised. Can we start over?"

"Start over? You ain't hear that Cardi B song, 'When It's Up, Then It's Up!' How the fuck you gone sell a bitch out and then ask a bitch for some help? Ain't no way—"

I reached out and grabbed her by the waist. I roughly pulled her into me and held her against me with both hands.

"Let me go, nigga! Crazy ass nigga! You must've lost your damn mind!"

She placed her hands on my chest and tried to push me back. I made my chest bounce in her hands, and she instantly pulled her hands back.

"Nigga, don't do that!"

"Listen…calm down…I need help, and I'll pay for it. Nothing crazy. Just hear me out. First things first, what's your name?"

"Get off me!" She put her hands on my chest and tried to push me again.

I made my chest bounce again, so she slapped my chest.

"Will you cut that shit out."

"Tell me your name and I'll let you go," I reasoned.

"Let me go, boy!"

"Name?"

She rolled her eyes and blurted, "Brandy! Damn nigga, now let me go!"

I slowly loosened my grip and let her back out of my arms.

"Crazy ass nigga, what's your name?"

"Bo-T."

"Well, what the hell do you want, Bo-T? I'm listening."

"Alright…look, I'm in a real fucked-up situation right now and I really need a place to crash. I really just wanna take a shower so I can really wash all these cuts and scars. After that, I wanna rest and then I'll be on my way…I'll give you a grand just to let me take a shower and a nap?" I questioned.

"Alright, I'll give you two grand."

"Shit…alright, muscle man, Bo-T…Where my money?" Brandy spoke with her hand out.

I reached into the pocket of my gym shorts and pushed my wad back out. I counted out twenty blue faces and stuffed the rest back in my pocket.

"Here," I stated while passing her the money.

"Alright now, keep on splurging like you ain't got no sense and yo ass gone end up broke. Looks like you bankroll getting slim," Brandy joked while accepting the money.

"Yeah, I doubt it, but I'll keep that in mind."

"Alright, I'll follow you, Bo-T," Brandy stated while walking around the black two-door Honda I had parked next to.

She hopped into her driver's seat and started her engine. I quickly jumped back inside my Jaguar and did the same. Next thing I know I was on the road and talking to a stranger.

***

When I got to Brandy's house, she led me straight to the bathroom and then went on about her business. All I had in my possession was an extra pair of boxers and socks I had brought in from the luggage bag in my back seat.

I scrubbed away all of it and grime that last night's rain failed to wash and then realized my muscles under the steaming hot water. Some of the cuts in my body had reopened and begun to bleed again but that was minor, the biggest pain I felt was coming from the center of my aching bones.

After my shower I put on the clean socks and boxers with the same gym shorts and then joined Brandy in her living room.

Brandy lived in a two-bedroom house and lived technically by herself. She had an older sister named Bambi that lived with her as well but was rarely home because she spent most of the time at her baby daddy's house. So, at the moment, it was only me and her.

Brandy quickly got me settled in on the couch with a pillow and a blanket and then disappeared down the hall that led to her two bedrooms and bathroom. I was still in a foreign place, but I could honestly say I felt much more comfortable on this couch, than I did in the alley behind the warehouse. I quickly went back to sleep while thinking about what I would do when I woke up.

***

When I woke up, my body was still sore but getting better. I sat up on the couch and stretched my arms and legs, cracked my back and looked around the living room.

There was a kitchen in the corner to my left, the front door was to my right, there was also a sliding glass door that led to the backyard on my left, and that was pretty much it. The living room had two couches, a small table in the center, and a forty-six-inch smart TV in front of me. The TV had a piece of paper taped to it and it seemed kind of odd, so I decided to check it out. It turned out to be a note.

I snatched the paper off of the TV and began reading.

Bo-T,

I had to go help my mama with a few things and by the time I get done with that I'll have to go to work. You seemed to be sleeping peacefully, so I decided not to disturb you. I held up my end of the bargain Hough, you got to shower, and you got a good sleep...Even though yo ass only said for a nap! LOL. But anyway, don't let my door hit ya where the good Lord split ya! And make sure my door is locked before you leave! You're welcome, muscle neck...

-Brandy-

After reading the note twice, there was only one thing I was sure of...And that was that by the time Brandy came home from work. I'd most definitely still be here!

I walked around the house and decided to get a better overall awareness of the layout. The garage had nothing in it, except for a bunch of tools and lawn care supplies. The kitchen was basically empty other than all of the basic appliances. Lots of plates and not enough food to put on them. The front and background appeared to be taken care of for the most part, and that really concluded the immediate surroundings around the living room.

I then walked into the long hallway with three doors at the end. The door directly at the end was the bathroom I had showered in last night, or this morning, depending on your perspective.

I stepped into the room on the right and looked around. The pink and white bedspread let me know the room belonged to a female, but I expected as much, since I already knew the only two people to inhabit this house were two females. The room didn't have anything in it worth mentioning and I didn't pry too deeply. I wasn't searching for anything, just looking around.

The room on the other side of the hall appeared to be exactly the same, but this room had come equipped with its own bathroom.

There were picture frames on the dresser of a skinny black woman that looked just like Brandy, so I assumed this was her sister's room.

I walked back into the other room and looked in the closet. I found what I was looking for on a hanger in the back of the closet. I pulled the red hoodie off of the hanger and threw it on. Of course, it was on the tight side since it belonged to Brandy, but it would still serve its purpose for the time being. I needed a hoodie to conceal myself while going inside the stores.

I exited the house and left the door unlocked since I didn't have a key. I hopped inside my ride and slowly made my way outside the neighborhood. I damn near forgot how to get to the entrance.

Once I was on the main road, I cruised around while looking for any sites that caught my interest. I ended up pulling over into a gas station and asking a black woman for help. She gave me directions to the nearest mall and then answered a few quick questions I asked her. I found out that I was in Savannah, GA. I was in unfamiliar territory and the realization of that became more and more apparent every time I turned down a new street.

When I made it to the mall, I pulled out two big wads of cash and then went on a small shopping spree. Nothing outrageous, but I got all of the things I needed and then grabbed as many outfits as I could carry. I definitely couldn’t let a bitch tha worked at Wendy’s shine on me. That would never happen again.

After the mall, I went to a barber shop. After that, I retraced my path back towards Brandy’s house and pulled over at the food market I saw in the plaza by her neighborhood. I wasn’t sure what type of food Brandy would prefer, but all black people eat certain shit, so I loaded up on all of the usual shit niggas crave for. I made a few laps around the food mart and ended up with two shopping carts overflowing with food. One cart was stacked with snacks and junk food and the other cart had straight food that needed to be prepared and cooked.

I then made my way back to Brandy’s house and stuffed her refrigerator and freezer to the point where the doors almost wouldn't shut. I filled the pantry and all of the cabinets with snacks and canned goods and put ten boxes of different cereal on top of the fridge.

I then grabbed a few hygiene items and then some comfortable clothes to wear and decided to take another shower. Once I was clean and smelling good, I stretched out on the couch and turned the television on, so I could watch the news. I looked at the watch I bought earlier and checked the time, 8:19 p.m.

I wasn't sure what time Brandy would be home but if she was expecting me to kick rocks, then she was in for a rude awakening. As far as I was concerned, I'd just found my new shelter.

Chapter 17

I ended up taking a nap, but I was fully awake by the time Brandy walked through the door in her Wendy's uniform a little after midnight. She took one look at me sitting on her couch, and immediately started running her mouth like I knew she would.

"Why they fuck is yo black ass still sitting up in my damn house?" Brandy blurted with her hand on her hip.

"I know you ain't calling nobody black." I laughed. "Yo purple ass way blacker than me! Matter of fact, I ain't even gone call you Brandy no more. From now, on I'm calling yo ass Purp!" I laughed some more.

"Alright, nigga, just sit yo ass right there and wait until I get back."

Brandy started down the hall and then turned into the room I knew was hers. Five minutes later, she slipped into the hallway bathroom and hopped into the shower. Twenty minutes after that, she slipped back into her bedroom and then made her way back into the living room and sat down next to me on the couch.

She was wearing some small pink shorts that seemed super pink compared to her shiny black skin, and a white tank top. Her ass looked even fatter now that it wasn't being restricted by pants, and the print in the front of her shorts I couldn't help but notice before she sat down, gave a whole new meaning to the word camel toe. Her D-cup breasts were full and perky, and I could clearly see her nipples and the big dark circles that surrounded them, since she wasn't wearing a bra.

I myself was chilling in a pair of Nike gym shorts and Nike socks…nothing else.

"I see you took yo nappy headed ass to the barber shop," Brandy commented.

"Yeah, I had to clean myself up," I replied.

"Alright, so the big question is, what the fuck you still doing here? I know you saw my note," Brandy spoke while pointing towards the television that no longer had her note taped to it.

"See what had happened was…"

"Sounds like you 'bout to be with the bullshit nigga."

"Naw, I really just want to thank you personally. You really helped me out and I can't feel comfortable leaving a note. I wanted to tell you personally, so I stepped out earlier and then I came back. I went to the mall to get some new gear and then I went food shopping and filled up yo poor ass refrigerator."

"You put food in my fridge?" Brandy questioned in disbelief.

She then jumped up and rushed into her kitchen. She immediately noticed the large variety of cereal boxes on top of the fridge and then quickly checked the rest of the kitchen. Every place she could think of was loaded to capacity.

"What are you tryna do?" Brandy questioned while reclaiming her seat.

"Just tryna show my appreciation to a beautiful woman. The only way I know how to do that is through my actions. I provide and I guarantee security," I spoke while leaning back.

Brandy stared at me through squinted eyes and said, "I ain't no damn trick, nigga. I ain't no thot hoe that fuck niggas for food and money! So, if you tryna trick a bitch out some pussy, you can save yo breath and bounce, nigga."

"If I thought you were a trick, and I wanted some pussy, then I would've told you that. You sound crazy. Instead of telling you I had two G's for a damn shower and a place to rest, I would have flashed my bank roll and asked you, What's up with that pussy?"

She realized I had a point and then said, "Yeah, I guess, but still…All niggas got a motive. Niggas don't give bitches money and fill they house up with food for nothing. Especially if they don't even know the bitch!"

"It ain't trickin if you got it," I stated with a grin.

"Oh, so you got it like that?"

"Didn't I tell you that when we met? Yo pocket watching ass think that baby ass knot I showed you was all I got? I hope I ain't dealing with a dummy."

"So now what do you want? You said thank you…okay, you're welcome, no problem. I appreciate the money, I really needed it, and I appreciate the food, as you can see, I needed that too. Now what?”

“Now I was hoping we could have a serious talk and work a few things out,” I stated honestly.

“Okay, what's up?”

“Alright, let me ask you a couple of questions that might play a big role in whatever I got in mind.”

“Go for it.”

“How old are you?”

“I'm twenty-four and you?”

“Thirty-four.”

“Old ass nigga,” Brandy laughed.

“Whatever, you got a nigga?”

“Yup.”

“Does he come over here?”

“Sometimes…Sometimes I go to him. We just got together, so we don't do too much.”

“Alright, other than working at Wendy's, what do you do?’

“Like what?”

“Do you work anywhere else? Do you go to school? Shit like that.”

“Nah, I work at Wendy’s, split the bills with my sister, and live life freely.”

“What type of life can you live with a Wendy's paycheck? All your money goes straight to your bills.”

“It's only temporary until I find something better, so I ain’t worried.”

“You could probably make way more money as a stripper with all that ass you got.”

“You got me fucked up! I ain't that type of bitch! I ain't got nothing against the women that do it, but that ain’t for me.”

“My bad, don't shoot me. Alright…well, without beating around the bush, I'm really tryna figure out how I can’t stay here a little longer. I still ain't got nowhere to go and I’d like to stay here. I know you.”

"Nigga, you sound stupid! You smoke crack? What kind of drugs are you on? I don't even know you, nigga! Not even a little bit! And you want me to move you into my house?"

"It's like having a roommate. A lot of people don't know their roommate until they move in…How much do you pay for half of the rent?"

"I pay four-fifty."

"What else do you pay?"

"The cable and water bill, my sister pays everything else."

"As long as you let me stay here, I'll cover all of your bills, no pressure. So now you can save all of your money or spend yo shit on whatever. You damn sho ain't gotta worry about another bill. You got my word on that."

"If you can do all of that, then why don't you just rent an apartment or get a hotel or something? I don't get it. Something ain't right about this, so you might as well just cut the bullshit and tell me what's up. And how the fuck I'ma move a nigga in my house, and I got a whole boyfriend right now? How does that look?"

"Alright, look…I'ma be real with you. I ain't even from round here and my situation crazy. Long story short, I got a couple warrants, serious warrants. I'm from Florida, when the police tried to arrest me, we got into a fight, then they shot at me and shot my lil brother. We ended up on a high-speed chase and I crashed. When I crashed, I flew out the windshield" I paused to read her expression and then I continued.

"Somehow, I still got away and drove here to Georgia. I been sleeping in my car the whole time, but I can't keep living like that and I can't do anything legit, because I'm a wanted man. I ain't no rapist or nothing like that. I'm just a real ass nigga that's been chasing a bag and I made a few mistakes along the way. I'm a street nigga from top to bottom and I get my money out the mud, so you know how that go.

"I met you by chance and other than the fact that you gotta face like Kelly Rowland and a body like Nicki Minaj, I like yo vibe. I know I talked a lot of shit when we met, we both did, and I can't say how you really feel. But me personally, I actually think you fine as fuck and funny as fuck. I can tell you from the gutta and I like ya vibe, baby. As far as yo boyfriend goes, shit, I ain't gone get in yo way. Anytime that nigga come over here just introduce me as yo big brother."

Brandy sat quiet for a moment while staring at me. She seems to be considering it, but also battling herself in her mind and trying to figure out if any of my offers were worth it. "So, what if the police came here looking for you?" Brandy questioned.

"They won't...The police don't know where I'm at and they ain't got no way of finding out. You know how this shit go"

"How long do you tryna stay?"

"I can't give you an exact time frame and I don't know. Right now, I just wanna take it day by day and figure shit out along the way. I wanna keep these crackas off my back, stay rich and get richer, and find my lil brother that got shot. Them the only plans I can count on."

"What happened to your lil brother?"

"That's a story for another time, right now we need to come to some sort of understanding. So, what are we gone do? Are you fucking with me?"

"I'm either the dumbest bitch in Savannah or the craziest, but yes, I'm fucking with you, Bo-T. And just for the record, I ain't mean none of that shit I said about you...except for all of the shit I said about that shirt yo ass had on. Yo ass was gone die if you wore that bitch any longer." Brandy laughed.

I laughed with her and then said, "Yeah...whatever, Purp. I bought me some new clothes today, so that ain't never gonna be another issue."

"Alright...well, I ain't gotta work tomorrow, so I guess we can use that time to get to know each other better. Right now, I'm tired and finna take my black ass to sleep," Brandy spoke while rising from the couch.

"You mean yo purple ass," I joked. "But alright, I'll holla at you later, whenever you get up then," I stated while staring at her queen-sized camel toe.

Brandy then turned on her heels and started back towards her room. Once she was gone, I laid back on the couch and closed my eyes.

Well, that worked out. Mission accomplished…I found a good spot to lay my head at…so now what?

Chapter 18

Over the next few weeks, I kicked it with Brandy, day in and day out, and we became surprisingly close. Her sister never came around, so we still hadn't met. I questioned why she paid half of the rent and bills for a home she never stayed in and Brandy told me that her baby daddy had told her he would continue to pay her bills if she moved in with him. So, her sister wasn't paying shit.

I did however end up meeting Brandy's boyfriend at some point, and the nigga turned out to be a straight green beat. The nigga was broke as fuck and I could tell he wasn't really in the streets like he said he was. He was actually one of the reasons why me and Brandy had become closer. After noting the major differences between me and him, how could she resist? I was wealthy, he was broke. I was built like a body builder, and he was out of shape and pudgy. I was a gangsta, he was a wanksta. No comparison, no competition,

She remained faithful though and didn't cheat on the nigga. I only took a shot at her once though. She came out of the bathroom butt ass naked one night, and tried to act like it was nothing. I tried to push up on her and she turned me down. I never tried her after that, but I was plotting.

I splurged a lot of money in her favor and put new furniture throughout her house. I got her a new wardrobe and was thinking about buying her a new car. All of my clothes and shit was in her room now and we took the Jaguar to the junkyard. Once she got a glimpse of my three treasure chests, she started acting like she had hit the lottery.

Tonight, Brandy wanted to get out of the house and somehow convinced me into going with her. She told me all of the best clubs and the most action took place around downtown in Atlanta. So, we got dressed for the occasion and then jumped inside Brandy's Honda and pulled off. After making the long drive to Atlanta, I decided I'd definitely be buying a new car within the next week. I'd just get something comfortable for the both of us.

I could tell Brandy wasn't used to dealing with niggas of my caliber because when we approached the club, and I headed straight for the door—fuck the line—she looked at me like I was crazy. I dropped a couple of blue faces in the hands of the bouncers and quickly headed inside of the club without being searched. Brandy was right on my arm.

"We could've got in the damn line, nigga. You always wasting money," Brandy spoke over the blaring music as we entered.

"I keep telling you, it ain't trickin if you got it," I responded while looking around.

The club was lit and crowded from wall to wall. One of Money Bagg's latest tracks was screaming through the club, and the song had everybody going nuts.

"Let's get something to drink," Brandy stated while guiding me towards the bar.

The bottle girl was a caramel-colored beauty with a small breast and a Buffie the Body booty. She looked me up and down from over the counter and took notice of my apparel. I was rocking a three-thousand-dollar Maison Margiela outfit, with a pair of red bottom Christian Louboutin's on my feet. My jewelry was shining, and my teeth were gleaming. My hair was wavy, and my full beard was neatly sculpted. My pockets were stuffed with Benji's and I know I smelled like money.

It wasn't naan other nigga in the building rocking Maison Margiela. I wasn't the only fly nigga in attendance by far. Shit, this was Atlanta! But I damn sho was putting on and letting my presence be known.

"Hey baby, what can I get your fine ass tonight?" the bottle girl asked me while licking her lips and boldly making her interest clear.

"What are my options?" I asked with a grin.

"You can get whatever you like, baby. And I mean whatever!"

Before I could respond to the flirtatious gesture, Brandy stepped in with a mug on her face and her arm around my waist while blurting, "give us a bottle of Dom Perignon and keep your eyes off my man!"

The bottle girl rolled her eyes and trotted off to get the bottle.

"So, I'm yo man now?" I joked to Brandy.

"A bitch ain't finna be all up in yo face while you with me. Call it what you want, but these hoes got me fucked up! Tonight, yo ass is off limits, nigga…play with it."

All I could do was laugh while the bottle girl brought us our bottle. She tried to hand me the bottle, but Brandy snatched it and dropped the payment on the counter. Brandy snatched me by the arm and turned me towards the crowd. I looked over my schedule and Brandy smacked me on the back of my head.

"Don't play with me, nigga! I'll go back and hit that hoe upside her head with this big ass bottle! Try me!" Brandy blurted while shaking her neck.

"Ease up, baby...you ain't gotta do all that. If you want me, I'm yours." I posed while wrapping my arm around her waist and pulling her into me." Stop acting like you don't know how I really feel about you," I whispered into her ear before placing a kiss on her cheek.

Brandy was smiling from ear to ear while popping the top on our bottle. Together, we drank out of the bottle while making our way towards the dance floor. We danced together for ten songs straight and she stayed clinging to me the entire time.

"I gotta go to the bathroom, baby," Brandy spoke.

"Alright, me too," I stated while following Brandy towards the bathrooms.

I stepped inside the men's room and went inside a stall to piss. While I was pissing, I heard the door open and then some niggas walked into the bathroom arguing.

"I ain't paying that nigga no fuckin thirty racks for one fuck ass brick! Fuck naw! Call that nigga back and tell that nigga I got twenty-five right now. Either take the quarter or I'm straight, fuck that nigga!" one of the dudes spoke.

"Big bag alert?" another nigga spoke.

"Real shit, bra, a nigga ain't got no more dope and now that it's time to re-up, this fuck nigga wanna raise the price on a nigga! That nigga trying us like some bitches!"

I flushed the toilet and stepped out of the stall. The two niggas got quiet and leaned against a wall while I washed my hands. While holding my hands with a paper towel I looked at my reflection in the mirror. I had to make sure everything was still on point.

I turned around and looked at the two niggas leaning up against the wall. They both looked like they were barely eighteen.

"I ain't tryna get in y'all business, but it sounds like y'all got a problem." I looked both of the young niggas in their eyes with a serious facial expression. "If you're interested, I have a solution to your problems."

The young niggas looked at each other and appeared to be wondering what to say.

"Well?" I spoke. "Time is money, I ain't got time to be playing."

"Alright, what are you talkin 'bout?" one of the youngins questioned.

"How much you paying for your work?" I questioned.

"I was paying twenty-three, but now my plug is asking for thirty! That's crazy!"

"Give me twenty-one and I got you," I stated

"Twenty-one? For a whole brick?" the youngin questioned with surprise.

"What, are you wearing with a wire or something, jit? Take your shirt off," I demanded.

"Take my shirt off? Fuck no! I ain't—"

I quickly whipped out my chrome .45 and held both of them niggas up at gunpoint from a distance. Both of them quickly thew their hands up and backed against the wall.

"Shirts off…Both of y'all," I demanded.

Both niggas quickly took their shirts off and dropped them to the floor.

"Tank tops off," I demanded.

They quickly snatched off their tank tops and dropped them on top of their shirts.

"Spin around," I ordered.

They both spun around slowly and I didn't see anything suspicious.

"Empty out them pockets," I ordered.

They quickly emptied their pockets on top of their shirts. They had a couple bands, phones, and car keys.

"Pick up your phone," I ordered the nigga that had done all of the talking so far.

He reached down to grab his phone and then stood up looking baffled.

"Take this number down." I recited the number to the new phone I had gotten last week. "Twenty-one a pop. If you're interested, call me. I ain't mean to shake you down like this, but sometimes you gotta make sure, especially these days. Get at me, jit."

I quickly backed out of the bathroom and bumped into Brandy as soon as I backed out. She noticed me putting my gun back into my pants and gave me a suspicious look. I grabbed her by the hand and led her back towards the front of the club.

"What's up, baby, you ready to slide? I'm getting kind of hungry," I spoke over the music.

"Alright, let's go. My feet are starting to hurt anyway," Brandy stated.

We exited the club hand in hand and made our way to the car. As soon as we settled in and zoomed off, my phone started ringing. I didn't recognize the number, so I ignored it. As soon as I ignored the call, the same number immediately called again.

"Yo!" I answered.

My phone was plugged into the radio playing music, so the call was being answered on the car speaker.

"What's good? Uh, this Malik, the nigga from the bathroom."

I instantly recognized the voice as the young nigga who I had just given my number to. Brandy looked at me with a raised eyebrow and then switched lanes.

What the fuck was she thinking?

"What's up, young nigga?" I asked while rubbing on Brandy's thick chocolate thigh.

"I just wanted to say it ain't no pressure on how that went down, and if everything's all good, then I'd like to make that happen for the price you gave me," Malik spoke. His voice sounded extra loud, booming through the speakers in the car.

"Alright, when you wanna do that?" I asked, brushing my fingers against Brandy's fat pussy.

Brandy kept her eyes on the road and kept driving but opened her legs to give me more access. She was wearing a thong and the thin string was being swallowed by her thick lips. I pulled the string out of her lips and moved it to the side. I began to slowly rub on her clit while leaning over the armrest and licking on her neck.

"Mmmmmm," Brandy moaned.

"Shit, I was hoping we could handle that tonight, if that's possible? Me and my dawg ain't from Atlanta, so we was hoping we could make that happen, before we headed back to our city," Malik spoke.

I damn near forgot that lil nigga was on the phone, now that I was sitting here with all of this pussy dripping in my hand.

"I don't stay in Atlanta either, but we can work something out though. You got all the money on deck right now?" I asked while pushing two fingers inside of Brandy's soaking wet tunnel.

"Mmmm, bae," Brandy moaned.

"What?" Malik blurted.

"I said, do you got the paper on deck right now?"

"Oh, yeah. That's why we tryna get up with you now."

"I stay in Savannah, so if you wanna make that drive right now, then I got you."

"Just give me an address and I'll jump on the road."

"I'ma text you where to meet me at in about five minutes. Be on point," I stated and then ended the call.

I went back to sucking on Brandy's neck and began pumping my fingers in and out of her with speed.

"You gone make me crash," Brandy moaned.

We were on the highway doing 80 mph on our way back to Savannah, but I couldn't care less. I was horny as fuck.

"You gone give me this pussy tonight?" I asked, still stroking her tunnel with my fingers, and rubbing her clit at the same time with my thumb.

Brandy had my whole hand soaking wet, and her pussy was making squishy noises.

"Yesss, baby," Brandy hissed.

"So, this is my pussy now?" I asked while picking up the pace.

"Yes, baby."

"You sure?"

"Yes, baby, yesss!"

"I don't like sharing," I barked.

"She's all yours, baby," Brandy moaned.

I suddenly pulled my fingers out of her pussy and stopped sucking on her neck. She looked at me like she couldn't believe I had just stopped, right when she was probably getting close to cumming.

"Call that square ass nigga you got right now and tell that nigga it's over," I ordered.

Brandy looked at me like I was crazy and said, "Nigga, really? I could've did that shit after my nut! What the fuck?"

"I'll wait," I responded.

"You gone fuck around and piss me off, and our relationship just fucking started, nigga," Brandy huffed. She picked up her phone and swiped her hand across the screen. "Call Josh," she blurted into her phone.

Her phone instantly found the name Josh stored in her contacts and made the call.

"What's up, bae?" Josh answered.

"Our relationship is over, nigga. Don't call me anymore, lose my number and forget about me, we're done," Brandy blurted into her phone and then hung up.

Her now ex-boyfriend immediately called her back, so I snatched her phone and answered.

"Don't make this harder than it has to be. Don't get yourself killed over a bitch that don't want you no more. Move on, playa, this fat ass pussy over here is under new management, so do yourself a favor and don't call back no more," I spoke and then hung up.

"Now come on, baby. Finish what you started," Brandy purred. "Trust me, baby, I got you."

Chapter 19

Brandy squirted in my hand and all over her seat three times, by the time we made it back to her house. She tried to jump on me as soon as we got into the house, but I had to let her know the money came first. I texted Malik and gave him the directions to the shopping plaza down the block from Brandy's house. Everything went smoothly with the transaction, so we locked in for future business.

When I got back in the house, I went straight to Brandy's room and threw the twenty-one bands inside my bag of money. I had a bag full of money, bag full of drugs, and a bag full of artillery. How could I lose?

When I stepped out of Brandy's room and turned, I collided with Brandy's sister in the hallway. I knew it was her because of the pictures I had seen.

"What the fuck? Who the fuck is you?" Bambi spoke. She quickly looked me up and down and then shouted towards the living room. "Brandy! Why the fuck you ain't tell me you had a nigga up in here?"

"Didn't know I had to!" Brandy screamed back.

"Well, who the fuck is he?" Bambi shouted.

"My new man!"

"Umph! You damn sho upgraded, bitch! This big chocolate nigga is what I call fine!"

"Keep yo eyes off my man, hoe!" Brandy shouted and rushed into the hallway "Bo-T get yo ass out here before I fuck you up!"

"Damn, baby! Easy-easy! I ain't even do anything," I stated.

"Bo-T, this is my sister, Bambi. Bambi, this my nigga, Bo-T. He stays here with me now," Brandy spoke while squeezing between us.

Brandy was so jealous and territorial, and it always made me laugh to see the way she acted about me. She always did the most and we just got together.

Shit, I ain't even given her the pipe yet!

"What's up, handsome?" Bambi spoke while looking at me.

"Keep your eyes above the neck!" Brandy blurted.

"Bitch, please! Yo nigga fine, but he yours, bitch! I'm just checking him out to see what you have done got yourself. And if his ass stays here, then his ass better be helping you pay some bills," Bambi spoke firmly.

"I'm actually what you call *that* nigga!" I spoke up. "I keep her happy, keep her spoiled, and I pay all of her bills" I stated with assurance.

"Oh, you done went and found you a breadwinner, Brandy! Okay, bitch! Do it big then, hoe!" Bambi laughed. "So, what's the catch? He fine as hell and he paid, so what…let me guess, he got a little dick?"

"You got my nigga fucked up, bitch! That's the total package right here. My nigga swinging like King Kong!" Brandy laughed.

"Do I need to confirm that?" I butted in.

Brandy slapped me on the side of my head and said, "Nigga, don't play with me! You ain't funny."

"Ease up, Purp…just a joke, baby." I laughed.

"Like I said, you ain't funny...Now come on!" Brandy blurted and grabbed me by my arm. "See you later, bitch! I'm about to climb Mount Everest!" she spoke over her shoulder to Bambi while dragging me into the bedroom.

Brandy pushed me onto the bed. "I been waiting all damn night on yo ass, nigga! Now stop playing and give me that dick!"

Brandy snatched my shorts off and then snatched off my boxers. My dick stood up like the Eiffel Tower and Brandy didn't hesitate to get what she wanted. She jumped on top of me and planted her feet flat on the bed beside my hips. She stared me in the eyes and slowly squatted down until the tip of my dick parted her slit.

When the head of my dick pushed into her opening, her jaw dropped, and she moaned, "Damn, nigga."

She continued to ease her way down and I could feel myself stretching her tight walls.

"It's so thick!" Brandy purred.

The moment she made it down to the base, her thighs started shaking and she came all over my lap.

"Fuck all this slow shit!" I blurted, "I'm about to give you what you asked for."

I grabbed her arms and pulled her forward, pulled her upper body down on top of me, and wrapped my arms around her back. Her lower body was still in a squat position and my dick was still buried in her tunnel. I then roughly thrust my hips upward and began pounding my dick into her pulsating pussy.

"Ohh, shit! Ohhh, shit! Fuck me, baby! Yes!" Brandy started shouting.

"That dick good, huh?" I grunted while keeping my strokes powerful.

"Yess! Nigga, yes!"

Brandy's pussy was gripping me like a hand and then the sound of our bodies slamming together was echoing throughout the room.

"Oooooh, fuck! Hold up, baby! Wait! Wait! I can't take no more!" Brandy screamed while creaming all over my dick.

"Shut yo black ass up and take this dick!" I grunted and started pounding her hard.

"I can't! I can't! I can't take any more! Fuck, baby! Fuck!"

I thrusted into her five more times, then exploded inside of her creamy wet guts.

"Damn!" I blurted and finally let her go.

Bandy fell to the side and started shaking. Her whole body appeared to be vibrating and her eyes were somewhere lost in the back of her head.

"I need a blunt," I blurted.

I rolled out of the bed and grabbed the open pound of weed I kept on the floor beside the dresser. I removed a pack of Backwoods from the top drawer and pulled it out. After I rolled and lit up, I sat back on the bed and slapped Brandy on the ass. She was dead to the world.

I put my shorts back on and stepped out the room. I slipped into the bathroom and took a quick piss while still puffing on my blunt. After I wiped my dick off and washed my hands, I stepped out of the bathroom and came face-to-face with Bambi. She was butt naked and smiling.

"Damn, nigga...you putting it down like that?" Bambi spoke.

"What are you talking about?" I questioned while stepping to the side and moving around her.

"You just gave that bitch the Holy Ghost! You think I ain't hear y'all? I'd have to be deaf not to hear that shit. It sounded like you might've been too much for her," Bambi lustfully spoke.

I looked down and got a good look at her small perky breasts. Her nipples poked out like Tootsie Rolls. I looked at them some more and trailed her tight slim stomach down to her slimmer waist and slim hips. I stopped at a wide gap between her legs and quickly came to the conclusion that fat ass pussies and super-sized camel toes just ran in the family.

"See something you like?" Bambi asked with her hand on her hips.

Man, what the fuck going on around this bitch?

"No comment," I replied and blew a cloud of smoke in her face.

She stepped past me and walked back into her bedroom. She left the door open and then crawled onto her bed, crawled to the center of her bed on all fours and arched her back. Her fat ass spread open and was already glistening wet.

Damn!

My feet grew a mind of their own and stepped inside her room. Before I knew it, I was on top of the bed behind Bambi and my shorts were on the floor in front of the bed. My dick was instantly back on brick, and I was rubbing the head up and down the slit of her opening. Her ass was small and bubbly, and I could fit her whole ass in the palm of my hands.

"Give it to me, nigga…get this pussy, baby," Bambi purred.

I pushed my dick into her super wet pussy and held her small cheeks firmly while sliding into her. When our bodies connected, I pulled back and then slammed into her again.

"Beat this pussy, baby! Don't play with it," Bambi moaned.

I grabbed her by her slim waist and gave her what she wanted. I started pounding her pussy hard and long.

"Yes, nigga! Just like that! Just like that! Just like that nigga! Beat this pussy! Beat this pussy! Pull my hair!"

I reached forward and snatched her hair back and pulled her head up. I pulled on her hair like I was pulling on the ropes of a sled and beat her pussy up like she wanted me to.

"Damn, nigga! Yes, nigga! Yesss! Fuck me! Fuck me!" Bambi shouted.

She was screaming so loud I started getting worried about Brandy waking up. I was fucking the hell out of this bitch with the door wide open! But fuck it...I was in too deep...literally! "I'm about to cum! I'm b'out to cum, nigga! Keep getting this pussy! Keep getting this pussy! Fuck!" Bambi shouted and then flooded my lap with silky water.

Two strokes later, I was busting my second nut of the night deep into Bambi's stomach. When I let go of her waist, she flopped forward and was breathing heavily. I looked down and noticed the whole section of bed in front of me was soaked. Some hoes were squirters, some hoes were creamers, this bitch was a hoser!

I slid off the bed and put my shorts back on. I grabbed my half-smoked Backwood and fired it back up. When I looked at Bambi, she was just like Brandy, dead to the world!

I just put two bitches to sleep back-to-back! I stepped out of her room and poked my head into Brandy's room. She was still knocked out. I slid into the bathroom and decided to clean myself up.

After a quick shower, I jumped back into my new bed with Brandy. I was feeling good and loving my new set-up. I went to sleep wondering how long I could keep this going.

Chapter 20

During the course of the next two months, things had gotten better and better. Brandy turned out to be my partner in crime. She stuck to me like glue, but I wasn't complaining. She showed me she had a gangsta side and held me down like a gutta bitch was supposed to.

Me and Bambi continued to fuck every chance we got, which wasn't easy with Brandy glued to my hip, but we managed to make it work. If Brandy was at work, we were fucking! If Brandy went to sleep, we were fucking! One time Bambi sucked my dick in the car while Brandy went into the store to pay for some gas! We made it work.

I met Bambi's baby daddy a couple of weeks ago. He started wondering when Bambi was spending more and more time away from him, in the house she didn't need and then became suspicious when he found out I lived there now. Lately, the nigga had been coming around much more often but he turned out to actually be a fool nigga. His name was KayDee and he was twenty-six, the same age as Bambi.

KayDee was about five-nine and somewhere around a hundred-sixty pounds. He was an average size nigga, but he carried himself aggressively, like he was a six-four nigga. He had just as many tattoos as me and had been to prison before, so his gangsta was certified. He was heavy in the dope game and quickly became one of my biggest customers. His only problem was being unaware of the fact that his baby mama was a straight up freak, and I was busting that hoe on a regular basis. I guess it can be like that sometimes.

Malik was a twenty-year-old wild nigga with a group of equally young wild niggas. Despite the way we met, jit respected the game and respected my gangsta. I plugged him and his niggas in and started serving his whole clique. They usually just patched up together and grabbed two or three blocks at a time. Between Malik, his niggas, and KayDee, I was eating good and didn't have to lift a finger.

At the present time, I was sitting on the couch in the living room smoking a blunt with KayDee. We had sent Brandy and Bambi off together to get their hair and nails done, so me and bra was just chilling in the meantime.

"This shit smoking, nigga! Where did you get this shit from?" KayDee asked me while passing me back the blunt.

"I had bought ten plates of this shit from a Jamaican nigga in Decatur," I replied while taking a pull of the blunt.

"You tryna step out tonight?" KayDee questioned in a low voice.

"Say what?" I asked.

This nigga KayDee had a bad habit of talking in a barely audible voice. The nigga had a voice like Keith Sweat, but his voice also had a slight rasp to it like the dead rapper, Pop Smoke.

"I said, you tryna step out tonight?" KayDee repeated in a slightly louder tone that was still barely understandable.

"What do you have in mind?" I questioned.

"Shit, I was thinking 'bout fucking off in one of them clubs in the A…maybe Onyx or Strokers."

"I ain't gone lie, I ain't really in the mood for all that shit. Every time I fall off in the strip club, I show my ass and do too much. I'm just tryna kick it tonight," I said.

"Alright…shit, well instead of blowing money, how about we step out tonight and make some money?" KayDee suggested.

"Shitttt, now you might be talking in my language...talk to me."

I got a lil play set up that I've been laying on. It's a simple in and out. All we gotta do is get the nigga to open the door and then blitz him…he keep all of his money in a safe, but if we shake him down hard enough, that green ass nigga gone give it up."

"Where is it at?"

"On the other side of town by Hitchville."

"When can we hit?"

"Shit, we can hit that bitch tonight! Soon as the sun go down, we can slide on that nigga."

"What's the profit?"

"I'm estimating anywhere between one or two hundred bands! Fifty-fifty split. The lick really sweet as fuck! It's a nigga I be serving. The nigga my sister baby daddy homeboy. I be serving both of them niggas but I ain't gone fuck with my sister baby daddy. I wouldn't take no food out of my sister mouth, but this other nigga fair game!"

"Sounds like a date," I decided. "We'll put some shit together and figure it out later. Right now, you need to pass that blunt."

The front door opened and then Brandy and Bambi walked into the house, looking super black and ghetto fabulous.

"Hey, baby!" Brandy blurted while jumping on my lap. "Look at my nails," she spoke while sticking her hands in my face.

"Fuck the nails, the first thing I noticed when you stepped through the door was the fact that you need to start handling all of your business at night. Yo extra black ass can't afford to spend no more time in the sun! Twenty more minutes outside and yo ass would've came in this bitch looking like a Goodyear tire!" I spoke while laughing.

Brandy popped me in the forehead with the palm of her hand and blurted, "Shut the fuck up! You think you funny, nigga...Give me a kiss."

I tongued Brandy down while gripping her ass cheeks and felt myself getting excited.

"Down, boy!" Brandy giggled.

"Get a damn room," Bambi blurted while rolling her eyes.

"That might be a good idea." Brandy giggled.

Bambi looked at me and I could sense the jealousy seeping through her pores.

"What's up, bae?" KayDee asked Bambi while pulling her down on the couch beside him.

"Nothing," Bambi said with an attitude.

"Let's order some food," Brandy suggested.

"What y'all wanna eat?" I asked everyone.

"Pizza!" Brandy blurted.

"Pizza sounds good," KayDee agreed.

"I want Chinese food!" Bambi blurted.

"Chinese food it is then," I decided.

Bambi smiled from ear to tear.

"What? Why the fuck she get what she want just like that? I want pizza, nigga! And KayDee agreed!" Brandy blurted.

"Easy, baby, easy! Whenever somebody say Chinese food, they automatically win! Don't nothing beat shrimp fried rice! Now when we are talking about ordering some shit" I explained.

Brandy poked her lips out and scrunched up her face.

"Don't do that…After we eat the Chinese food, I'll make you my dessert," I stated while kissing Brandy on the cheek.

Brandy instantly cheered up.

"You gon eat the cake?" Brandy purred.

"Damn right! Right after I lick the icing," I replied with a grin.

"I'ma rub that icing all over yo lips, nigga," Brandy spoke.

"Can we order the damn food!" Bambi blurted.

"I'll order it up," KayDee spoke.

"Thanks, brother," Brandy said to KayDee.

"No problem, sis," KayDee spoke while making the call.

***

"Pull up right here," KayDee directed.

I pulled up to the house he pointed to and then parked on the curb by the mailbox.

"You wanna kill 'im or let him live?" I questioned.

"It really don't matter, but if we let him live, we can probably rob him again when he powers back up," KayDee reasoned.

"It matters because that decision will determine how we play this," I spoke.

"What do you think?"

"This yo lick, man! You the one that know the nigga! I got all the props we'll need, however you wanna do it. Just make a choice and I'll tell you how we gone play it."

"Let him live," KayDee decided.

"Say less. Put this on then," I stated while passing him a ski mask from my backseat.

I explained to him how we would go in and kept it simple. I then put a ski mask over my head as well but rolled it up like a skully. I grabbed a bottle of ketchup I had brought just for the occasion and then dumped a couple of globs onto my shirt. I smeared some on my neck and then exited the car.

KayDee skipped beside me, and we quickly approached the house that was about fifty yards away on the corner. KayDee ran past me and crouched down beside the front door, behind a rocking chair. I then roughly banged on the door and kept banging until the nigga answered.

"Man, who the fuck banging on my shit?" a male voice shouted from inside the house.

A tall dark-skinned male snatched the door open, with a big .44 Magnum revolver in his hand and blurted, "What the fuck you—"

"Help me! Help me, please! I just got shot!" I coughed and then fell facedown in the doorway.

He never got a good look at my face, but he saw all of the ketchup all over my shirt and hands and shouted, "Oh, shit! Just keep breathing, bra! I'll call 9-1-1!"

The nigga jetted back inside his house and scrambled towards his couch in his living room. I pulled my ski mask down and then jumped to my feet like a cat. KayDee had already blitzed through the front door with his AK-47 firmly gripped in both of his hands. KayDee waved the stick from side to side but nobody else was in the room.

The tall nigga had grabbed his phone off the couch and was just turning around when KayDee kicked him square in his back and sent him crashing over the armrest. KayDee then hit him in the side of his head with his stick and then jammed his barrel right up against his forehead.

"Move, and I'll blow yo shit off," KayDee barked.

I quickly approached the nigga and snatched the .44 Magnum off the floor where he had dropped it. I stuffed the big revolver in my waistline and then slapped him upside his head with my .45 for good measure.

"Whatever you niggas want, just take it! Just don't kill me, man, please!" the nigga pleaded.

"Shut yo soft ass up!" I blurted. "Now tell me where the sack at, before I fuck yo soft ass up!"

"Room down the hall on the left! My safe is in the closet!"

"What's the code?" KayDee barked.

The nigga just looked at KayDee and didn't speak.

Wham!

I instantly slapped him in the nose with my .45 and shouted, "Answer the question, fuck nigga!"

"Ahh, fuck!" the nigga shouted. "I didn't hear what he said!"

"I said, what's the code, fuck nigga!" KayDee growled.

The nigga looked at KayDee frantically, but still didn't speak.

Wham!

"Is you deaf, dumb, or stupid? Answer the question before I smoke up!" I then pointed my pistol at the center of his face and barked, "Last chance, nigga!"

"I don't even know what he said!" the nigga cried. "I can't hear him!"

I looked at KayDee and burst out laughing. Turn the volume up, nigga! We ain't auditioning for a movie! We hitting a lick, nigga! Speak up so this nigga can hear you!"

"What's the code, pussy nigga? Quit playing, fool!" KayDee barked and popped him in the head with the back of his stick.

"Five-fifteen-twenty-six!"

I swung the bedroom door open that I was directed to, and immediately dropped down, with my pistol sweeping left to right. The rooms were empty. I ran to the closet and found the safe as promised. I punched in the code and hit the jackpot. The last time I hit a nigga safe, I hit the jackpot forreal, but this was still good.

I snatched a pillowcase off one of the pillows and loaded it up with money. That was all the safe consisted of. Piles of money. I then looked around and didn't see anything else of value in my eyes, so I left the room and speed walked back into the living room.

"Where the dope at?" I blurted to the tall nigga still jammed up at gunpoint with blood leaking down his face.

"Tell me a lie and we will smoke yo bitch ass."

"Washing machine in the garage," the nigga said sadly.

"Where the fuck that's at?" I blurted.

The nigga pointed towards a door in the corner, and I immediately skipped off in that direction. I quickly found the washing machine on the other side of the door and searched it thoroughly. I found about eighteen ounces of coke inside a bag wrapped up in a sweater. I kept looking and didn't find anything else. I checked the dryer just for the hell of it and came up empty.

"How much work did you get?" I questioned when I re-enter the living room.

"About a half of a block," the nigga replied.

I looked at KayDee and he nodded his head.

"Soft ass, petty hustling ass, fuck nigga!" I blurted. I swung the pillowcase over my back and said to KayDee, "Let's ride, nigga!"

I ran out the house and jetted straight for the car. KayDee slowly walked backwards while keeping his stick trained on the tall nigga. He stopped in the doorway and waited for me to bring the car around.

I honked the horn while pulling up to the house. KayDee shook the AK-47 like he was about to let it rip and the tall nigga flinched.

"Scary ass nigga," KayDee stated and then sprinted towards the car.

When he dove in the passenger seat, I swerved off and swerved us back to my spot. It didn't take long to get home and when I stepped through the door, I immediately took off my dirty, ketchup-stained clothes and headed towards the bathroom. After a quick shower, I returned to the living room where KayDee was patiently waiting for me.

"Let's count this loot." I told KayDee to keep the dope. I was sitting on so many bricks, I didn't need that petty ass hit.

KayDee took his half of the block and threw it all inside a book bag. He then got up and headed towards Bambi's room. I rolled up a blunt and then walked into the room I shared with Brandy. I'd sleep good tonight, knowing I had just made a free fifty-six G's!

Chapter 21

I hadn't seen Bambi or KayDee in about a month, but me and Brandy were with each other all day, every day. I usually dreaded being crowded by hoes, but Brandy is always so hyped up and funny that I never got tired of her company. She also had the wettest pussy I'd ever had. Other than Bambi's.

I was standing on the porch when Brandy pulled up in the new all-white 2020 Audi I bought her three months ago. She parked and hopped out with the Taco Bell I had sent her to pick up, and we entered the house together.

I sat down on the couch and immediately attacked my XXL Chalupa and Nacho Bell Grande, while Brandy ran off in the bedroom to take her clothes off. I was fucking up two Dorito shelled tacos when she joined me on the couch. She had a bottle of Absolut Vodka in her hand and swiftly uncapped the top. She took the lid off the large fruit punch drink that came with my order and poured the liquor into the large cup. I had drunk about half of the fruit punch, so she poured until the cup was full.

"I wanna have drunk sex tonight," Brandy stated while mixing the fruit punch and liquor with a straw.

"Shit, you ain't saying nothing. Let's take some shots," I said.

I filled the cup up with liquor and quickly knocked down the shot. I filled it back up and then passed it to Brandy. She knocked the shot down like a champ, and then I repeated the rotation three more times. After four shots apiece, we sipped on the fruit-punch-flavored vodka and started laughing and playing with each other.

My phone started ringing, so I quickly snatched it up off of the table and blurted, "Yoo!"

"What's good, big bra?" Malik spoke through the phone.

"What's up, jit, talk to me," I spoke louder than necessary because of the alcohol.

"I'm tryna pull up and blow a bag, big bro! You know how I do."

"Throw some numbers at me."

"Sixty-three."

"Pull up to the house," I stated and hung up.

"Who was that?" Brandy asked.

"Them lil niggas, Malik them. Jit finna pull up and cop shit."

Brandy started rubbing on my face and rubbing on my chest.

"Alright now," I spoke. "I'll fuck around and give you what you looking for."

"Well, stop playing and give it to me then," Brandy slurred. "Matter of fact…lay back…I got this."

I leaned back on the couch and lifted my hips while Brandy tugged my shorts down. She got down on her knees in front of me and positioned herself between my legs. Brandy rubbed her hands up my thighs and leaned forward, slurped my dick up into her mouth and sucked on my head like a Blow Pop. She rubbed her hands over my abs while slowly working her jaw muscles.

"Mmmm," Brandy hummed.

I threw my hands behind my head and enjoyed the view. Brandy knew how to work her mouth and she was never lazy. She put passion into it and did the most every time.

She grabbed my balls with one hand and massaged them, stroking my shaft with the other. She quickly put me back into her mouth and sucked me straight into the back of her throat. She didn't have a gag reflex, so her face dropped straight into my lap. She bounced her head up and down and slurped me up from top to bottom.

"Bust on my face, baby," Brandy moaned while stroking me with her hands.

I stood to my feet and grabbed the back of Brandy's head with both hands, pumped my dick in and out of her throat like I was fucking her pussy. I pounded her face for ten minutes straight and she didn't even mind. She just stared into my eyes the entire time while I was drilling her.

I felt my nut rising and kept stroking her face. I then stuffed my dick into her as deep as I could manage. Her lips were on my body and her nose was jammed against my pubic hairs. My eyes rolled into the back of my head and my toes curled up on the carpet. I bust my nut deep into the bottom of her throat and held her head in place to fill her throat up with semen.

When my dick stopped throbbing and my toes uncurled, I let go of her head and dropped back onto the couch. Brandy slurred. "You don't know how to listen."

"My bad, Purp…that throat was feeling so damn good I couldn't help it."

"Mmmmhhh...I got something for yo hard-headed ass. Sit on the floor," she ordered while climbing off of me.

I slid off the couch and flopped onto the floor, reached forward and grabbed my cup of liquor off the table and took a giant gulp. I was so drunk now I didn't even feel the burn. I put the cup back on the table and leaned back against the couch, while sitting on the floor.

"Lay yo head back," Brandy instructed.

I leaned my head back on the seat of the couch and waited for my next instructions. No further instructions came through and I didn't need any understand what was up and to handle my business. Brandy threw her legs over my head and straddled my face. She lowered her thick glistening pussy over my mouth and moaned, "Sssss...yesss, baby…suck on this pussy, baby."

I wrapped my arms around her thighs and held her firmly while parting her fat lips with my tongue. I sucked her throbbing clit into my mouth and hummed into her body.

"Yess, baby, damn…eat the cake, baby…slap my ass!"

I let go of one of her thighs and slapped her hard on the ass. Her ass cheek slapped and bounced against my face, and I slapped it again. I then used both of my hands to massage her soft juicy ass cheeks while devouring her kitty.

"You ready for the loving, baby?" Brandy moaned.

I answered her question by sucking her clit back into my mouth. That was all took for her to cream all over my face. Her body shook and vibrated, and her head tilted back with her mouth wide open. She rubbed her pussy all over my face and spread her cream all over me.

"Nigga, I love you!" Brandy blurted. "You bet not ever let another bitch sit on this mouth! You belong to me, nigga!" she slurred while still rubbing and grinding her pussy all over my lips.

My phone started ringing again, so she hopped off of me and let me answer it.

“Yoo!” I drunkenly shouted.

“We are outside, big bra!” Mike blurted.

“Oh, shit! Alright!” I hung up. “I forgot these lil niggas were on their way,” I slurred. “Yo freaky ass distracted me. Put yo shorts back on! Hurry up!” I shouted to Brandy.

I quickly dashed into the bathroom and washed my face. This black ass had her creamy ass nut all over the damn place. When I re-entered the living room, Brandy was sitting on the couch with her legs folded up under her silly ass and she stuck her tongue out at me.

I opened the front door and stepped to the side to let Malik in. Malik stepped past me and entered the house, along with three of his homies that I knew fairly well by now. The nigga Bag Alert was the nigga with Malik in the bathroom the day I met them. Bank Roll was Bag Alert’s lil brother, and the fourth nigga was named Rone that came around from time to time.

I usually made Brandy get the orders ready in the bedroom and had her hand it to me when I walked in, so she was never seen drugging my transaction, but tonight we were on some drunk shit, so fuck it. These lil niggas weren’t a threat anyway. That's why I only served them and KayDee.

Everybody looked at Brandy, but nobody spoke. Malik handed me a book bag and told me to count it up. His money was always on point, so I didn't have to check it. Sometimes I would, most times I wouldn't.

I gave Brandy the bag and whispered in her ear, “Go grab a three-piece.”

She didn't reply. She simply wobbled to her feet and obeyed my command.

“What you niggas got going on tonight?” I asked the group of youngins.

“We ain’t doing nothing but chasing paper,” Malik shouted.

“Big bag alert!” BankRoll echoed.

I looked at Rone to see what kind of funny shit he would say and of all the shit to say, this nigga asked me if he could use the bathroom. Apparently, the ride from their city had his bladder about to burst. I pointed him down the wall and told him which door to enter. I watched him walk into the bathroom and shut the doors.

Brandy quickly stumbled back into the living room, laughing like somebody had just told a joke, and tossed me the same bag I had handed her. She flopped down onto the couch and covered her mouth, like that would stop her crazy ass from giggling. I looked in the bag and peeped that Brandy had removed all the money, and replaced it with the three kilos I had instructed her to grab. Even though she was wasted, she was on point.

Rone came back into the living room, right as I was tossing the bag back to Malik. Malik quickly peeked inside the bag and then nodded his head with approval. I dapped the four young niggas up aggressively, due to my drunk state of mind and ushered them out the door.

"What the fuck is you steady laughing about?" I asked Brandy after locking the door and sliding down next to her on the couch.

Brandy looked at me and started laughing harder. Her laughing made me laugh, but I really wanted to know what the fuck she was laughing for.

"Helloo…Earth to Brandy! What the fuck is so funny?"

"When I was coming down the hall and I looked at you, I thought…damn, my nigga got a damn soccer ball head!" Brandy burst out laughing." Now every time I look at you, I see a soccer ball!"

"Oh, you wanna ride?" I laughed. "Yo ass."

A key rattling in the front door grabbed my attention and as I turned my head to look up, the front door opened and Bambi and KayDee walked in.

"Well, damn! Hey, strangers!" Brandy blurted.

Bambi locked the door and said, "Oh whatever, bitch! Hey, Bo-T."

"What's good?" I spoke.

"What do they do?" KayDee spoke.

"Huh?" I questioned.

"What do they do?" KayDee repeated.

"Another day, another dollar," I replied.

"Y'all motherfuckas drunk as fuck!" Bambi blurted. "Pour me up!"

"Help yourself," Brandy spoke.

Bambi quickly skipped into the kitchen and grabbed herself a cup full of ice. She returned into the living room and filled her cup up with vodka. She took a big sip and scrunched her face up.

"Damn!" Bambi blurted and passed her cup to KayDee.

KayDee took a gulp and scrunched his face up too. "That shit burn like a bitch," KayDee repeated.

"Who are you talking to?" Brandy asked KayDee.

"I'm talking in general," KayDee responded.

"What?" Brandy asked KayDee.

"I'm talking in general," KayDee replied.

"What?" Brandy questioned.

"Man, bro…Can't nobody hear that shit, nigga! One supper cool ass nigga. We in this bitch drunk as fuck and you wanna come up in this bitch whispering and shit! Come on, bra…stop it," I blurted.

"Ain't nobody whispering, nigga. Y'all drunk ass just can't hear me because y'all drunk!" KayDee blurted. He then looked at Bambi and said, "You can hear me just fine, can't you?"

"What?" Bambi asked.

"Now you wanna join the bullshit? I ain't got time for y'all. Y'all wanna be funny." KayDee took another gulp of the liquor and then passed the cup back to Bambi. "I'm finna go lay down." KayDee strode down the hallway and vanished into Bambi's room.

"What y'all bout to do?" Bambi questioned while sipping her drink.

"Shit, I ain't got no plans. I'm just coolin. What you wanna do?" I asked Brandy.

"I wanna cream all over that dick and then lay down and watch a movie with my nigga," Brandy replied.

"Sounds like a plan to me." I smiled.

"That's all you ever want to do, bitch! Keep yo ass tooted in the air and shit. I ain't tryna hear that tonight. It be sounding like yo ass be 'bout to die when y'all fuck!" Bambi spoke.

"I be 'bout to die and go to heaven!" Brandy blushed.

"Whatever, bitch," Bambi stated and rolled her eyes. She looked at me like she wanted to cuss me out and punch me in my face.

"I'm going to my room. If I'm lucky I'll see you later, Bo-T."

"Bitch, what you mean by that?" Brandy shouted.

"That means if you don't put the nigga to sleep then maybe he will smoke one with me later…damn, hoe, chill out," Bambi spoke and winked at me.

Brandy didn't see the wink and said, "Oh, alright…well, bye! We 'bout to get busy."

Bambi rolled her eyes again and stormed off towards her bedroom. Brandy then clumsily climbed on top of me and began sucking on my neck.

"Where were we?" she whispered in my ear.

Me and Brandy did exactly what she wanted to do. We fucked like wild drunk animals and then cuddled up together on the couch and watched a *Netflix* movie, I don't know what the hell we were watching, but as soon as the movie started, the liquor and the sex knocked me out and put me to sleep.

Chapter 22

"Ahhh!" Bambi shouted and tried to jump up from the couch.

Brandy screamed and the sudden movements instantly woke me up from my drunken slumber. I quickly realized why she was screaming as I jumped up and I couldn't believe my eyes.

"Nobody moves, nobody gets hurt," some nigga spoke, with a pistol aimed directly at me and Brandy.

I had never seen this nigga before a day in my life, but I knew he meant business, because this young ass nigga had the nerve to be standing in my living room, pointing a gun at me bare faced. My mind instantly started coming up with defense strategies. I was empty-handed at that moment, but I had my .45 sitting on the small table in front of me and I always kept my lifesaving MAC-90 underneath the couch.

Before I could register another thought, the sound of glass shattering diverted my attention. Out of nowhere, some fat nigga flew through the sliding glass door and stood next to the nigga that had me stuck to the couch. The nigga didn't flinch.

"You good?" the fat nigga asked the nigga with the pistol.

"Yeah, I got it," the nigga answered.

The fat nigga then shot down the hall out of sight. I kept my eyes trained on the nigga in front of me and kept going over different options in my head. Brandy seemed to be doing the same thing. I heard some voices coming from the hallway and couldn't believe somebody else was actually in my shit.

Boom!

An extremely loud gunshot suddenly erupted in the hallway and the first thing I thought about was Bambi. The nigga that had me pinned down to the couch seemed to be disturbed by the sudden gunshot, and turned his head with a confused look on his face. As far I was concerned, it was now or never and that was my cue to make a move.

I leaped off the couch and snatched my .45 off the table, while diving to the floor behind the other couch like an Olympic swimmer.

Boom! Boom!

The young nigga took two wild shots at me while stepping forward.

Boom! Boom!

Two loud shots rang out in the hallway again and I didn't have a single clue as to what the fuck was going on! I don't know if this was a robbery, a hit, or both!

Tat-Tat-Tat-Tat-Tat-Tat-Tat-Tat-Tat-Tat!

Oh, shit!

Brandy never let me down. She had gotten her hands on the MAC-90 underneath the couch and let that bitch rip! She was doing a pump faking! I lifted my head up and saw the nigga that thought he had us down bad, sprint towards the shattered back glass door and dive outside into the grass. My ears were ringing, and I was still trying to make sense of what the fuck was happening.

I didn't see anything or hear anything else, so I called out, "Brandy?"

"Yeah, baby?" Brandy blurted back.

"You good?"

I stood up and quickly looked around. Everything was quiet.

"Get up, Purp!" I spoke to Brandy.

Brandy rose from the couch, with the MAC-90 clutched in her hands and quickly swung it around the room, while looking like a female GI Joe.

"Stay on point…let's check the back," I spoke.

I crept up to the corner of the hallway and peeked around the side. The fat nigga that had burst through the sliding glass door, was lying flat on his back in front of Bambi's bedroom door with blood everywhere. I motioned for Brandy to watch my back and follow me into the hall.

We quickly strode to the end of the hall, and I noticed all three doors swerved open. I quickly swung right, and Brandy swung left. We scanned both of the bedrooms at the same time.

"Oh my God!" Brandy screamed.

I was looking at the open window in my bedroom when Brandy screamed, so I instantly turned around to see what was happening.

Brandy dropped the MAC-90 and ran into Bambi's bedroom. Bambi was sitting on the floor crying with KayDee's lifeless head laying in her lap.

Bambi was rocking back and forth on the floor and crying, repeating, "I love you, baby! I love you!"

I kneeled down and saw all the blood pouring from KayDee's dead body.

"What happened?" Brandy blurted.

"We were laying down and heard some glass break. KayDee got up and grabbed the .44 Bo-T gave him and stood by the door, trying to hear if anything was wrong," Bambi sobbed. "The door swung open and that boy in the hallway tried to run in, so KayDee shot him! Then somebody from y'all room shot KayDee twice and disappeared. My baby just died right in my arms!" Bambi cried.

"Who the fuck is this?" I asked and pointed to the fat nigga sprawled out in the hallway.

"I don't know, baby," Brandy sobbed.

"What about you, Bambi? Get yo ass up and look at this nigga!" I ordered.

Bambi wiped her tears and laid KayDee's dead head on the floor. She rose to her feet and walked to the door. "I don't know him," Bambi spoke through her tears.

I started hearing the unforgettable sound of police sirens in the distance. Somebody in the neighborhood probably reported the in-house gunshots.

"Brandy the police probably about to show up and you know like I know when they get here, I can't be here! I'm about to take the car and duck off somewhere. When the police come, handle the situation. Nigga broke in the house and tried to rob KayDee, he tried to hold down the fort, nigga ended up dead. You know how to play it, y'all gone be good…Now hurry up and help me get everything illegal out of here. Them crackas might search this shit, so we need to hurry up and clean this shit up!" I quickly spoke.

Brandy jumped to her feet and didn't hesitate to help me make trip after trip and load the car. Bambi just sat on the floor crying the whole time. Once the car was fully loaded with all of my drugs, guns, and money, I turned to Brandy and passionately stuck my tongue in her mouth.

"I love you, baby!" Brandy cried.

"I'll be back, Purp, just chill. Get these crackas from around here and call me when the coast is clear," I stated.

"Let me come with you, baby! Please!" Brandy crowed.

"Ease up, Purp! I'll be back! Just get this shit under control and call me. I'll probably get a room for the night. I don't know yet. Worst-case scenario, I'll come back to get you and we'll buy a new house. Either way, I ain't gonna leave you, baby."

The sirens got louder, so I jumped in the car and quickly zoomed away. I swerved out of the neighborhood while thinking about what just happened.

What the fuck?

If it ain't one thing it's always another. Bad luck always got a way of finding me. I mean shit, technically I was straight. I ain't lose shit, product-wise, but I may have possibly just lost my safe haven. and at the moment a safe haven was what I needed the most!

I bent a couple corners while thinking about who just tried to rob me. Common sense told me it was them young niggas I be serving, because the niggas that ran up in my shit seemed to be about the same age. Even though I had never seen the intruders before, I had to classify them as niggas that rolled with the nigga Malik somehow. Guilty or innocent, Malik had to get it. I wasn't about to let that shit slide.

I ended up whipping the Audi into the parking lot of a low-budget motel. I put a hat on my head and lowered the brim, then got out of the car and trotted into the front office to see if I could get a room for a few nights.

When I walked in, an older white man was sitting behind the desk, watching a small TV. The older man looked up and smiled.

"Hey there, son, how can I help you?" the man asked with a deep country accent.

"I need a room for a few nights and all I've got is cash. No credit card, no ID, none of that…just cold hard cash," I spoke.

"Well, son, cold hard cash has always sounded good to me. How many nights are we talking?"

"How much for a week? I probably only need a couple of days, but a solid week should cover me."

"That would normally run you about three-fifty, including the deposit, but since you say you—"

"Here goes seven hundred! I like my privacy." I reached into my pocket and pulled out a wad of cash. I slapped seven bills on the counter and the old man quickly snatched them up.

"Let me get you a key," the old man spoke while moving quickly.

He handed me a key card and then told me how to get to my new room. I thanked the man and quickly made my exit. I hopped back into my ride and pulled around the building towards the back where my room was. After packing, I entered the room and then locked the door behind me.

I sat down on the stiff bed and looked around the small room. Shit was always changing up in the blink of an eye. Hopefully, Brandy got everything under control soon and hopefully, everything went smoothly. Would probably have to still move anyway, just because now her house would have a whole lot of attention on it that I definitely didn't want.

I rolled up a fat blunt and laid back on the bed while plotting on my future moves. I had a few things in mind, but I needed to clear my mind and figure out how I would make it all work.

Chapter 23

When I woke up the next morning, I had a headache and a hangover. I left my room and rode down the street to a McDonald's. I ordered five McGriddles and some orange juice. After I smashed the breakfast sandwiches and swallowed my orange juice, I drove back to my motel room and sparked up a blunt.

Brandy called me and told me everything had gone as well as expected. The police had shown up and took statements from her and Bambi. They bagged the bodies up and took pictures. They did the usual police shit and then left without caring that two black men had killed each other during a home invasion. I told her I'd stay where I was for the rest of the week, just to make sure nothing flaky was going on. She tried to force me into picking her up so she could be with me, but I told her to sit right and chill out. I needed space to think a few things through. I told her I would pick her up in a couple of days and then we could find a new place to stay. She still had the Honda, so she would be fine without me in the meantime.

I called Malik just to see how he would play his hand and surprisingly, he played his like a professional. The nigga didn't seem to be showing any signs of a nigga that had something to hide. I decided to throw a curveball into the mix and told him I wanted to front him an additional three blocks to go along with the three he had copped yesterday.

Malik was either dumb as fuck, or he really didn't have anything to do with what happened last night. He jumped at the opportunity and told me he had shit going on today, so we made plans to link up tomorrow. I told him I was on the move, so I'd come to him to drop off the work when the time came. I wasn't sure how I would do it yet, but I knew I would somehow find the opportunity to blow that nigga candle out.

My phone went off while I was thinking of a master plan, and it was Brandy again.

"Alright nah, don't make me turn my phone off," I answered.

"Shut up, nigga! I'm hungry!" Brandy retorted.

"You got a refrigerator full of shit! Get yo lazy ass up and cook something!" I snapped.

"Baby, I want some Chinese food though! Chinese food always wins, remember?"

"Okay…get some Chinese then!"

"You took all of the damn money, baby. I ain't got nothing but ten dollas in my purse! You gotta come get me!"

I shook my head and said, "You playin, right?"

"Forreal, baby!"

I could see the smile on her face from way over here. Brandy had more tricks than that silly rabbit on the Trix cereal box. She was determined to stay up under me and for some reason, I decided fuck it, why not?

"Man, meet me in the plaza on the corner of yo block. Yo extra crispy ass better be there in twenty minutes," I declared.

"I'll be there in two!" Brandy shouted and hung up.

I laid back on the bed and laughed. I wanted for about five minutes and then I headed out the door. I made my way towards the plaza by Brandy's house, while debating whether or not I should bring her with me or just give her some money and pull off. As soon as I pulled up next to Brandy's Honda, she jumped out and quickly found her way into my passenger seat.

"Drive, nigga, drive! Hurry up!" Brandy shouted.

Something about the eagerness and urgency in her tone made me hit the gas and quickly burn rubber. I started to frantically look in every direction while thinking something was wrong.

After driving for about ten minutes in silence with my head on swivel, I realized the coast was clear. I put us on a route towards the nearest Chinese restaurant and looked at Brandy like she was stupid.

"Why the fuck you jumping in the car acting all paranoid and shit, and telling me to hurry up and pull off?"

Brandy had a big smile on her face when she responded. "So yo ass couldn't try to leave me there. Nigga, you ain't slick! And now you gone have to knock me out or kill me if you wanna get me away from you!"

Brandy had more tricks than a prostitute in Vegas! I pulled up to a Chinese spot and sent Brandy inside to place our orders and grab the food.

I should pull off on this hoe!

She eventually came back to the car with a big bag of take-out and dropped her fat ass butt back in the passenger seat. As soon as I pulled off, I decided to bring Brandy with me back to the motel. She had made my options very clear, and I knew she meant every word. That meant if I wanted to drop her ass back off, then I would have to either knock the bitch out or kill her! I ain't got time for that type of shit and her company ain't bad anyway, so fuck it.

I just hope this bitch ready to ride or die with a nigga like me!

As soon as we made it inside the hotel, we sat on the bed and dug into our food. I could probably live off straight Chinese food. My phone then rang and interrupted my grub session.

"Yoo!" I answered without even looking to see who called.

"Damn, big bro! I just seen yo house on the news! They say somebody tried to run off in your shit and got smashed! But they also said the home invader had smacked one of the residents in the process. Damn, bra! At first, I assumed the worst, but then I realized the news story was just a recap of some shit that happened last night. I just seen yo ass yesterday and I just talked to you earlier! Why yo ain't say nothin about that shit? The news ain't give me no names or nothing, though. Do you know who them niggas was? Damn, big bro! What happened? Just say the word and me and my niggas will slide!" Malik blurted through the phone.

Maybe this lil nigga really ain't have nothing to do with that shit.

"I'm just tryna figure shit out right now. I ain't sweatin nothing right now. That shit was something I ain't have shit to do with. Shit kinda hot though. That's way I said I'll come to you tomorrow," I said.

"Alright…damn, bro…just hit me up tomorrow then."

"Say less." I ended the call.

For the rest of the day and night, I fucked the air out of Brandy and plotted on what I'd do to Malik tomorrow. Whether he was in that shit or not, didn't even matter anymore. Somebody had to be held accountable for what happened, and that person was going to be him!

Chapter 24

When I woke up the following morning, I took Brandy's spoiled ass to a food spot she had woke up craving for and then I set up the play with Malik. Me and Brandy smoked a few blunts and kicked back inside the motel room for the whole day until nightfall approached. Under the clock of the night, Brandy joined me in the Audi and together, we zoomed off for our destination, which was Malik's house.

Brandy knew the play and she was done with the bullshit. In her eyes, it was her home that had gotten violated in all of the action, and she was ready for whatever.

I still had all of my shit in the car, so naturally I had a whole gun store in the backseat. In my lap I had my trusty Springfield .45, and on my hip, I had a big bore Desert Eagle. Brandy chose to roll with the MAC-90 and that was fine by me. She had already proven to me she could handle it. Brandy said holding the MAC made her pussy wet.

Brandy's role was to remain in the car anyway and then to bust in when the action started going down. That meant concealing the MAC wasn't an issue.

Brandy rolled up a blunt and then put it in rotation while we rode through the night, listening to a mixture of old Boosie, Webbie, Yo Gotti, Kevin Gates, Lil Baby, and Future.

I wasn't really paying attention as to whether or not I was driving fast or slow. But two hours later, I was pulling right up to the address Malik had given me. I pulled out my phone and gave him a call.

"What's up, big bro?" Malik answered.

"I'm outside, nigga, I just pulled up," I spoke.

"Slide on it, bra! Me and the squad got a spade game going right now. We are right here in the living room, so just walk in."

"Say less," I concluded. I looked at Brandy and said, "Stay in the car. When you hear the fireworks, join the party! If you catch anybody tryna break for it, break em off! Smoke everybody but me!

I want every last one of these niggas! I don't know how many niggas up in here, but we ain't leaving until we get all of them! I went inside and set it up. I'll call you if anything changes. Don't fuck nothing up!"

Brandy sat in her seat quietly with her game face on. She held the MAC tightly and nodded her head as I walked away from the car, with an empty book bag on my back.

I had my .45 tucked on my slide. Both pistols were clearly noticeable, and I didn't bother attempting to conceal them as I walked straight into the house. The air inside the house was thick and clouded with weed smoke, and Malik and the other niggas were sitting at table right in front of me playing cards. One of the niggas I had never seen before, and the other two niggas was Bag Alert and his lil brother Bank Roll.

"What's good, big bro?" Malik greeted while slamming down a card and then scooping up the four cards in the center of the table.

"What's up, lil nigga...what you niggas got going on?" I questioned the group while approaching the table.,

"Shit, we are just doing a little friendly gambling. Hundred a game," Malik spoke. "You want next?"

"Not for no hundred," I spoke.

"What you wanna do then? Two hundred a game?" Malik questioned.

"You act like y'all playing Tunk or Poker or some shit! I ain't finna play no long ass spade game for two hundred petty ass dollars! If you want me at the table, try ten stacks a game!" I spoke.

I could've blown all of these niggas' candles out right there with no problem. I could tell they were all strapped, but since I had the element of surprise, I could've dusted at least two of these niggas off, and then shot a third before getting into a bang-out with the fourth. The only reason I ain't make that option a reality was because me and Brandy had decided I should see if I could jack these niggas while we were here. I had just served these niggas three blocks the day before, so I could probably get that back or whatever was left of it, which should be most if not all. And I also should be able to get some money up off these niggas. I had to check the trap and see how it played out.

"Ten G's a game?" Malik questioned in a shocked voice.

"Big bag alert!" Bag Alert blurted.

"Bank Roll, bankroll!" Bank Roll echoed.

"Damn right! Don't tell me you niggas broke?" I laughed.

"Hell naw! You just surprised me with that amount. Shit, we are just kicking the bobo and friendly gambling. You act like we are in Vegas!" Malik spoke.

"Ain't no such thing as friendly gambling, nigga! So, what you young ass niggas wanna do? Either we go to some good money around, or I can just drop the bag off and go on about my business. I told you before, time is money, I ain't got no time to be playing, lil nigga," I explained.

"What do you wanna do?" Malik asked his partner, Bag Alert.

"Big bag alert!" Bag Alert replied.

I don't think I've ever heard that nigga say anything else the whole time I've known him. That nigga had to be retarded or some shit.

"Shit…let's do it then! Who will your partner be?" Malik asked.

"My partner in the car…We playing money on the wood jit! Drop them bands on the table and I'll tell my partner come in," I spoke.

"Alright, nigga. I'll be right back then," Malik stated, rising from the table.

"Let me holla at you while you're at it," I spoke, following him towards the back of the house.

I was going to follow this nigga to the stash and then stick his dumb ass up, but right before we bent the corner into a hallway, Malik's phone started ringing. While this phone was ringing, my phone was ringing at the same time. I checked my screen and saw it was Brandy.

What the fuck this girl want?

I quickly answered the phone and said, "What's up?"

“I don’t know what’s going on at your end, but a car just pulled up with three more niggas and they’re just sitting there. It looks kind of flaky,” Brandy explained.

While listening to her, I used my other ear to listen to Malik and heard him telling whoever he was on the phone with, to just walk in because the door was open.

“It’s all good, it's just going to be a bigger party tonight! But I'm doing something important right now, so be on point! I’m tryna make this quick,” I spoke to Bandy and then hung up before she could speak.

While putting my phone back in my pocket, I saw the front door swing open and then the nigga Rone stumbled into the house, looking scared. Either his clumsy ass tripped while stepping through the door, or somebody had pushed him. Malik had bent the corner into the hallway and right as I was about to follow him, a gunshot went off and then Rone’s head burst open like a watermelon!

Oh shit! What the fuck?

Boom!

Boom! Boom!

Bang! Bang! Bang!

Boom!

Bang!

Gunshots were going off in the living room I was just standing in like it was the Fourth of July!

“What the fuck going on?” Malik shouted and then ran in front of me to look around the corner into the living room.

I knew the lick had just somehow been ruined, so I aimed my .45 at the back of Malik’s head and pulled the trigger.

Boom!

Malik’s head blew up like a bag of popcorn, and blood and brains instantly splashed all over the wall and floor. His body dropped in front of me, and I stepped over him to peek into the living room.

Bang! Bang! Bang! Bang!

Boom! Boom! Boom!

I quickly ducked down so I wouldn't get hit by a stray bullet and just as I ducked, a chunk of the wall above me exploded and I was pelted with drywall.

Man, what the fuck kind of shit did I just walk into?

It suddenly just registered in my mind that one of the niggas I saw shooting when I peeked around the corner, was the same bitch ass nigga that had broken into my house the other night and had me held down at gunpoint.

I knew that fuck nigga was connected to these niggas! But why were they smoking each other?

Bang! Bang!

Boom! Boom! Boom!

Somebody suddenly dove into the hallway I was in and crashed right into me. I quickly smashed the nigga on the top of his head with the butt of my .45 and pushed him off me. I jumped to my feet and put two cannon balls into his face. That's when I realized the nigga I had just smoked was the lil nigga, Bank Roll.

I looked around the corner again and saw Bag Alert sprawled out dead, and the other nigga playing spades that I didn't know was hiding behind one of the couches, holding his stomach and bleeding badly. I kept scanning the battlefield and saw the nigga that tried to rob me leaning against the other couch and he was bleeding too, but he was alive and alert.

Me and that nigga locked eyes and then he shouted, "It's another nigga in the hallway, big bra!"

"Can you get 'em?" a familiar voice shouted back at the nigga from a hidden position in the living room.

Tat-Tat-Tat-Tat-Tat-Tat-Tat-Tat-Tat-Tat!

The nigga that tried to rob me that night, his whole body just did the Harlem Shake right before my eyes and half of his face flew off. Brandy played through the front door while putting the MAC-90 to use with no hesitation.

"Baby!" Brandy screamed while looking around wildly. The nigga hiding behind the couch holding his stomach had suddenly slumped over and died from the wounds he had accumulated during the gun battle.

"Baby!" Brandy screamed again, while slowly stepping further into the house with the MAC-90 raised high.

Boom! Boom!

Brandy's head snapped back, and her body flew into the living room wall.

"Brandy!" I shouted while leaping forward and diving behind a knocked over table.

I pulled out my Desert Eagle and now had a pistol in both hands. I was ready for an all-out war! I didn't realize until this very moment how much I truly cared about Brandy. Looking at her headless body brought an instant uncontrollable tear to my eye.

"Fuck!" I shouted in anger.

"That must've been yo bitch? Gone step out here so I can lay you down next to that bitch! Bitch ass nigga!" that familiar voice shouted from a location I couldn't pinpoint.

I quickly did the math and came to the conclusion that whoever this nigga was, he was the only nigga left standing. It was just me and him, and I didn't give a fuck about nothing at this point. My adrenaline was sky high, and I was pissed off!

"It's just me and you, pussy nigga! What you wanna do? I'm ready for whatever, fuck nigga! I'm ready to die right now!" I screamed while clutching my cannons.

"Bitch ass nigga! You ain't saying nothing! We can take this shit back to the Western days and Wild-Wild West in this bitch, fuck nigga!"

"Well, pop out then!" I shouted.

"Bitch ass nigga, you pop out!"

"Pop out on three, fuck nigga!"

"One!" the nigga shouted.

"Two!" I shouted back.

"Three!" we shouted in unison.

I jumped up like a Jack in The Box from behind the knocked-over table and saw a nigga already standing up behind a couch and aiming straight at me.

Bang! Bang!

Boom! Boom!

Our guns went off at the same time and I quickly dropped back down behind the table.

What the fuck? Am I trippin?

We had both missed our shots by inches, but what was really on my mind? I had to be seriously trippin out right now! I couldn't afford to be trippin like this in the middle of a fucking bang out! I'm in the middle of a life-or-death situation, and I'm over here seeing shit!

I shook my head and took a deep breath. A long moment passed and neither of us said anything. Next thing I knew, I heard something that made me lose my fucking mind!

"Skee-man! Please, tell me I'm hallucinating!" There it was, the all-too familiar voice I was currently in the middle of a shoot-out with.

"Skeecho!" I shouted back in complete disbelief. "Skeecho!" I shouted again with more assurance.

"Bo-T!"

I jumped up from behind the table I was crouched behind and stared my lil brother Wizz dead in his eyes. Tears instantly fell from my eyes and a smile spread across my face. All of my anger was instantly gone.

Get the fuck out of here!

To Be Continued…
Here Today, Gone Tomorrow 3
Coming Soon

Lock Down Publications and Ca$h Presents assisted publishing packages.

BASIC PACKAGE $499
Editing
Cover Design
Formatting

UPGRADED PACKAGE $800
Typing
Editing
Cover Design
Formatting

ADVANCE PACKAGE $1,200
Typing
Editing
Cover Design
Formatting
Copyright registration
Proofreading
Upload book to Amazon

LDP SUPREME PACKAGE $1,500
Typing
Editing
Cover Design
Formatting
Copyright registration
Proofreading
Set up Amazon account
Upload book to Amazon
Advertise on LDP Amazon and Facebook page

***Other services available upon request. Additional charges may apply

Lock Down Publications
P.O. Box 944
Stockbridge, GA 30281-9998
Phone # 470 303-9761

Submission Guideline

Submit the first three chapters of your completed manuscript to ldpsubmissions@gmail.com, subject line: Your book's title. The manuscript must be in a .doc file and sent as an attachment. Document should be in Times New Roman, double spaced and in size 12 font. Also, provide your synopsis and full contact information. If sending multiple submissions, they must each be in a separate email.

Have a story but no way to send it electronically? You can still submit to LDP/Ca$h Presents. Send in the first three chapters, written or typed, of your completed manuscript to:

LDP: Submissions Dept
Po Box 944
Stockbridge, Ga 30281

DO NOT send original manuscript. Must be a duplicate.

Provide your synopsis and a cover letter containing your full contact information.

Thanks for considering LDP and Ca$h Presents.

NEW RELEASES

SUPER GREMLINS 2 by KING RIO

LOYALTY IS EVERYTHING 3 by MOLOTTI

HERE TODAY, GONE TOMORROW 2 by FLY ROCK

Coming Soon from Lock Down Publications/Ca$h Presents

BLOOD OF A BOSS **VI**

SHADOWS OF THE GAME II

TRAP BASTARD II

By **Askari**

LOYAL TO THE GAME **IV**

By **T.J. & Jelissa**

TRUE SAVAGE **VIII**

MIDNIGHT CARTEL IV

DOPE BOY MAGIC IV

CITY OF KINGZ III

NIGHTMARE ON SILENT AVE II

THE PLUG OF LIL MEXICO III

CLASSIC CITY II

By **Chris Green**

BLAST FOR ME **III**

A SAVAGE DOPEBOY III

CUTTHROAT MAFIA III

DUFFLE BAG CARTEL VII

HEARTLESS GOON VI

By **Ghost**

A HUSTLER'S DECEIT III

KILL ZONE II

BAE BELONGS TO ME III

TIL DEATH II

By **Aryanna**

KING OF THE TRAP III

By **T.J. Edwards**

GORILLAZ IN THE BAY V

3X KRAZY III

STRAIGHT BEAST MODE III

De'Kari

KINGPIN KILLAZ IV

STREET KINGS III

PAID IN BLOOD III

CARTEL KILLAZ IV

DOPE GODS III

Hood Rich

SINS OF A HUSTLA II

ASAD

YAYO V

Bred In The Game 2

S. Allen

THE STREETS WILL TALK II

By Yolanda Moore

SON OF A DOPE FIEND III

HEAVEN GOT A GHETTO III

SKI MASK MONEY III

By Renta

LOYALTY AIN'T PROMISED III

By Keith Williams

I'M NOTHING WITHOUT HIS LOVE II

SINS OF A THUG II

TO THE THUG I LOVED BEFORE II

IN A HUSTLER I TRUST II

By Monet Dragun

QUIET MONEY IV

EXTENDED CLIP III

THUG LIFE IV

By **Trai'Quan**

THE STREETS MADE ME IV

By **Larry D. Wright**

IF YOU CROSS ME ONCE III

ANGEL V

By **Anthony Fields**

THE STREETS WILL NEVER CLOSE IV

By K'ajji

HARD AND RUTHLESS III

KILLA KOUNTY IV

By Khufu

MONEY GAME III

By Smoove Dolla

JACK BOYS VS DOPE BOYS IV

A GANGSTA'S QUR'AN V

COKE GIRLZ II

COKE BOYS II

LIFE OF A SAVAGE V

CHI'RAQ GANGSTAS V

SOSA GANG IV

BRONX SAVAGES II

BODYMORE KINGPINS II

BLOOD OF A GOON II

By Romell Tukes

MURDA WAS THE CASE III

Elijah R. Freeman

AN UNFORESEEN LOVE IV

BABY, I'M WINTERTIME COLD III

By **Meesha**

QUEEN OF THE ZOO III

By **Black Migo**

KING KILLA II

By Vincent "Vitto" Holloway

BETRAYAL OF A THUG III

By Fre$h

THE BIRTH OF A GANGSTER IV

By Delmont Player

TREAL LOVE II

By Le'Monica Jackson

FOR THE LOVE OF BLOOD IV

By Jamel Mitchell

RAN OFF ON DA PLUG II

By Paper Boi Rari

HOOD CONSIGLIERE III

By Keese

PRETTY GIRLS DO NASTY THINGS II

By Nicole Goosby

LOVE IN THE TRENCHES II

By Corey Robinson

FOREVER GANGSTA III

By Adrian Dulan

SUPER GREMLIN III

By King Rio

CRIME BOSS II

Playa Ray

HERE TODAY GONE TOMORROW III

By Fly Rock

REAL G'S MOVE IN SILENCE II

By Von Diesel

GRIMEY WAYS IV

By Ray Vinci

BLOOD AND GAMES II

By King Dream

THE BLACK DIAMOND CARTEL II

By SayNoMore

<u>Available Now</u>

RESTRAINING ORDER **I & II**

By **CA$H & Coffee**

LOVE KNOWS NO BOUNDARIES **I II & III**

By **Coffee**

RAISED AS A GOON I, II, III & IV

BRED BY THE SLUMS I, II, III

BLAST FOR ME I & II

ROTTEN TO THE CORE I II III

A BRONX TALE I, II, III

DUFFLE BAG CARTEL I II III IV V VI

HEARTLESS GOON I II III IV V

A SAVAGE DOPEBOY I II

DRUG LORDS I II III

CUTTHROAT MAFIA I II

KING OF THE TRENCHES

By **Ghost**

LAY IT DOWN **I & II**

LAST OF A DYING BREED I II

BLOOD STAINS OF A SHOTTA I & II III

By **Jamaica**

LOYAL TO THE GAME I II III

LIFE OF SIN I, II III

By **TJ & Jelissa**

BLOODY COMMAS I & II

SKI MASK CARTEL I II & III

KING OF NEW YORK I II,III IV V

RISE TO POWER I II III

COKE KINGS I II III IV V

BORN HEARTLESS I II III IV

KING OF THE TRAP I II

By **T.J. Edwards**

IF LOVING HIM IS WRONG…I & II

LOVE ME EVEN WHEN IT HURTS I II III

By **Jelissa**

WHEN THE STREETS CLAP BACK I & II III

THE HEART OF A SAVAGE I II III IV

MONEY MAFIA I II

LOYAL TO THE SOIL I II III

By **Jibril Williams**

A DISTINGUISHED THUG STOLE MY HEART I II & III

LOVE SHOULDN'T HURT I II III IV

RENEGADE BOYS I II III IV

PAID IN KARMA I II III

SAVAGE STORMS I II III

AN UNFORESEEN LOVE I II III

BABY, I'M WINTERTIME COLD I II

By **Meesha**

A GANGSTER'S CODE I &, II III

A GANGSTER'S SYN I II III

THE SAVAGE LIFE I II III

CHAINED TO THE STREETS I II III

BLOOD ON THE MONEY I II III

A GANGSTA'S PAIN I II III

By J-Blunt

PUSH IT TO THE LIMIT

By **Bre' Hayes**

BLOOD OF A BOSS **I, II, III, IV, V**

SHADOWS OF THE GAME

TRAP BASTARD

By **Askari**

THE STREETS BLEED MURDER **I, II & III**

THE HEART OF A GANGSTA I II& III

By **Jerry Jackson**

CUM FOR ME I II III IV V VI VII VIII

An **LDP Erotica Collaboration**

BRIDE OF A HUSTLA **I II & II**

THE FETTI GIRLS **I, II& III**

CORRUPTED BY A GANGSTA I, II III, IV

BLINDED BY HIS LOVE

THE PRICE YOU PAY FOR LOVE I, II ,III

DOPE GIRL MAGIC I II III

By **Destiny Skai**

WHEN A GOOD GIRL GOES BAD

By **Adrienne**

THE COST OF LOYALTY I II III

By Kweli

A GANGSTER'S REVENGE **I II III & IV**

THE BOSS MAN'S DAUGHTERS I II III IV V

A SAVAGE LOVE **I & II**

BAE BELONGS TO ME I II

A HUSTLER'S DECEIT I, II, III

WHAT BAD BITCHES DO I, II, III

SOUL OF A MONSTER I II III

KILL ZONE

A DOPE BOY'S QUEEN I II III

TIL DEATH

By **Aryanna**

A KINGPIN'S AMBITON

A KINGPIN'S AMBITION **II**

I MURDER FOR THE DOUGH

By **Ambitious**

TRUE SAVAGE I II III IV V VI VII

DOPE BOY MAGIC I, II, III

MIDNIGHT CARTEL I II III

CITY OF KINGZ I II

NIGHTMARE ON SILENT AVE

THE PLUG OF LIL MEXICO I II

CLASSIC CITY

By **Chris Green**

A DOPEBOY'S PRAYER

By **Eddie "Wolf" Lee**

THE KING CARTEL **I, II & III**

By **Frank Gresham**

THESE NIGGAS AIN'T LOYAL **I, II & III**

By **Nikki Tee**

GANGSTA SHYT **I II &III**

By **CATO**

PAID IN BLOOD **I II**

CARTEL KILLAZ I II III

DOPE GODS I II

By **Hood Rich**

LIPSTICK KILLAH **I, II, III**

CRIME OF PASSION I II & III

FRIEND OR FOE I II III

By **Mimi**

STEADY MOBBN' **I, II, III**

THE STREETS STAINED MY SOUL I II III

By **Marcellus Allen**

WHO SHOT YA **I, II, III**

SON OF A DOPE FIEND I II

HEAVEN GOT A GHETTO I II

SKI MASK MONEY I II

Renta

GORILLAZ IN THE BAY **I II III IV**

TEARS OF A GANGSTA I II

3X KRAZY I II

STRAIGHT BEAST MODE I II

DE'KARI

TRIGGADALE I II III

MURDAROBER WAS THE CASE I II

Elijah R. Freeman

GOD BLESS THE TRAPPERS I, II, III

THESE SCANDALOUS STREETS I, II, III

FEAR MY GANGSTA I, II, III IV, V

THESE STREETS DON'T LOVE NOBODY I, II

BURY ME A G I, II, III, IV, V

A GANGSTA'S EMPIRE I, II, III, IV

THE DOPEMAN'S BODYGAURD I II

THE REALEST KILLAZ I II III

THE LAST OF THE OGS I II III

Tranay Adams

THE STREETS ARE CALLING

Duquie Wilson

MARRIED TO A BOSS I II III

By Destiny Skai & Chris Green

KINGZ OF THE GAME I II III IV V VI VII

CRIME BOSS

Playa Ray

SLAUGHTER GANG I II III

RUTHLESS HEART I II III

By Willie Slaughter

FUK SHYT

By Blakk Diamond

DON'T F#CK WITH MY HEART I II

By Linnea

ADDICTED TO THE DRAMA I II III

IN THE ARM OF HIS BOSS II

By Jamila

YAYO I II III IV

A SHOOTER'S AMBITION I II

BRED IN THE GAME

By S. Allen

TRAP GOD I II III

RICH $AVAGE I II III

MONEY IN THE GRAVE I II III

By Martell Troublesome Bolden

FOREVER GANGSTA I II

GLOCKS ON SATIN SHEETS I II

By Adrian Dulan

TOE TAGZ I II III IV

LEVELS TO THIS SHYT I II

IT'S JUST ME AND YOU I II

By Ah'Million

KINGPIN DREAMS I II III

RAN OFF ON DA PLUG

By Paper Boi Rari

CONFESSIONS OF A GANGSTA I II III IV

CONFESSIONS OF A JACKBOY I II III

By Nicholas Lock

I'M NOTHING WITHOUT HIS LOVE

SINS OF A THUG

TO THE THUG I LOVED BEFORE

A GANGSTA SAVED XMAS

IN A HUSTLER I TRUST

By Monet Dragun

CAUGHT UP IN THE LIFE I II III

THE STREETS NEVER LET GO I II III

By Robert Baptiste

NEW TO THE GAME I II III

MONEY, MURDER & MEMORIES I II III

By **Malik D. Rice**

LIFE OF A SAVAGE I II III IV

A GANGSTA'S QUR'AN I II III IV

MURDA SEASON I II III

GANGLAND CARTEL I II III

CHI'RAQ GANGSTAS I II III IV

KILLERS ON ELM STREET I II III

JACK BOYZ N DA BRONX I II III

A DOPEBOY'S DREAM I II III

JACK BOYS VS DOPE BOYS I II III

COKE GIRLZ

COKE BOYS

SOSA GANG I II III

BRONX SAVAGES

BODYMORE KINGPINS

BLOOD OF A GOON

By Romell Tukes

LOYALTY AIN'T PROMISED I II

By Keith Williams

QUIET MONEY I II III

THUG LIFE I II III

EXTENDED CLIP I II

A GANGSTA'S PARADISE

By **Trai'Quan**

THE STREETS MADE ME I II III

By **Larry D. Wright**

THE ULTIMATE SACRIFICE I, II, III, IV, V, VI

KHADIFI

IF YOU CROSS ME ONCE I II

ANGEL I II III IV

IN THE BLINK OF AN EYE

By **Anthony Fields**

THE LIFE OF A HOOD STAR

By Ca$h & Rashia Wilson

THE STREETS WILL NEVER CLOSE I II III

By K'ajji

CREAM I II III

THE STREETS WILL TALK

By Yolanda Moore

NIGHTMARES OF A HUSTLA I II III

BLOOD AND GAMES

By King Dream

CONCRETE KILLA I II III

VICIOUS LOYALTY I II III

By Kingpen

HARD AND RUTHLESS I II

MOB TOWN 251

THE BILLIONAIRE BENTLEYS I II III

REAL G'S MOVE IN SILENCE

By Von Diesel

GHOST MOB

Stilloan Robinson

MOB TIES I II III IV V VI

SOUL OF A HUSTLER, HEART OF A KILLER I II III

GORILLAZ IN THE TRENCHES I II III

THE BLACK DIAMOND CARTEL

By SayNoMore

BODYMORE MURDERLAND I II III

THE BIRTH OF A GANGSTER I II III

By Delmont Player

FOR THE LOVE OF A BOSS

By C. D. Blue

MOBBED UP I II III IV

THE BRICK MAN I II III IV V

THE COCAINE PRINCESS I II III IV V VI VII VIII IX X

SUPER GREMLIN I II

By King Rio

KILLA KOUNTY I II III IV

By Khufu

MONEY GAME I II

By Smoove Dolla

A GANGSTA'S KARMA I II III

By FLAME

KING OF THE TRENCHES I II III

by **GHOST & TRANAY ADAMS**

QUEEN OF THE ZOO I II

By **Black Migo**

GRIMEY WAYS I II III

By Ray Vinci

XMAS WITH AN ATL SHOOTER

By Ca$h & Destiny Skai

KING KILLA

By Vincent "Vitto" Holloway

BETRAYAL OF A THUG I II

By Fre$h

THE MURDER QUEENS I II III

By Michael Gallon

TREAL LOVE

By Le'Monica Jackson

FOR THE LOVE OF BLOOD I II III

By Jamel Mitchell

HOOD CONSIGLIERE I II

By Keese

PROTÉGÉ OF A LEGEND I II III

LOVE IN THE TRENCHES

By Corey Robinson

BORN IN THE GRAVE I II III

By Self Made Tay

MOAN IN MY MOUTH

SANCTIFIED AND HORNY

By XTASY

TORN BETWEEN A GANGSTER AND A GENTLEMAN

By J-BLUNT & Miss Kim

LOYALTY IS EVERYTHING I II III

Molotti

HERE TODAY GONE TOMORROW I II

By Fly Rock

PILLOW PRINCESS

By S. Hawkins

NAÏVE TO THE STREETS

WOMEN LIE MEN LIE I II III

GIRLS FALL LIKE DOMINOS

STACK BEFORE YOU SPURLGE

FIFTY SHADES OF SNOW I II III

By A. Roy Milligan

SALUTE MY SAVAGERY I II

By Fumiya Payne

BOOKS BY LDP'S CEO, CA$H

TRUST IN NO MAN

TRUST IN NO MAN 2

TRUST IN NO MAN 3

BONDED BY BLOOD

SHORTY GOT A THUG

THUGS CRY

THUGS CRY 2

THUGS CRY 3

TRUST NO BITCH

TRUST NO BITCH 2

TRUST NO BITCH 3

TIL MY CASKET DROPS

RESTRAINING ORDER

RESTRAINING ORDER 2

IN LOVE WITH A CONVICT

LIFE OF A HOOD STAR

XMAS WITH AN ATL SHOOTER

www.ingramcontent.com/pod-product-compliance
Lightning Source LLC
LaVergne TN
LVHW020714110826
845149LV00012B/2262

9781960993243